Henry G. Smith

Gems and Precious Stones

with descriptions of their distinctive properties, the methods for

determining them, &c

Henry G. Smith

Gems and Precious Stones
with descriptions of their distinctive properties, the methods for determining them,
&c

ISBN/EAN: 9783337777562

Printed in Europe, USA, Canada, Australia, Japan

Cover: Foto ©Andreas Hilbeck / pixelio.de

More available books at **www.hansebooks.com**

TECHNICAL EDUCATION SERIES, No. 11.

DEPARTMENT OF PUBLIC INSTRUCTION

EDUCATION BRANCH.—J. H. MAIDEN, F.L.S., &c., *Superintendent.*

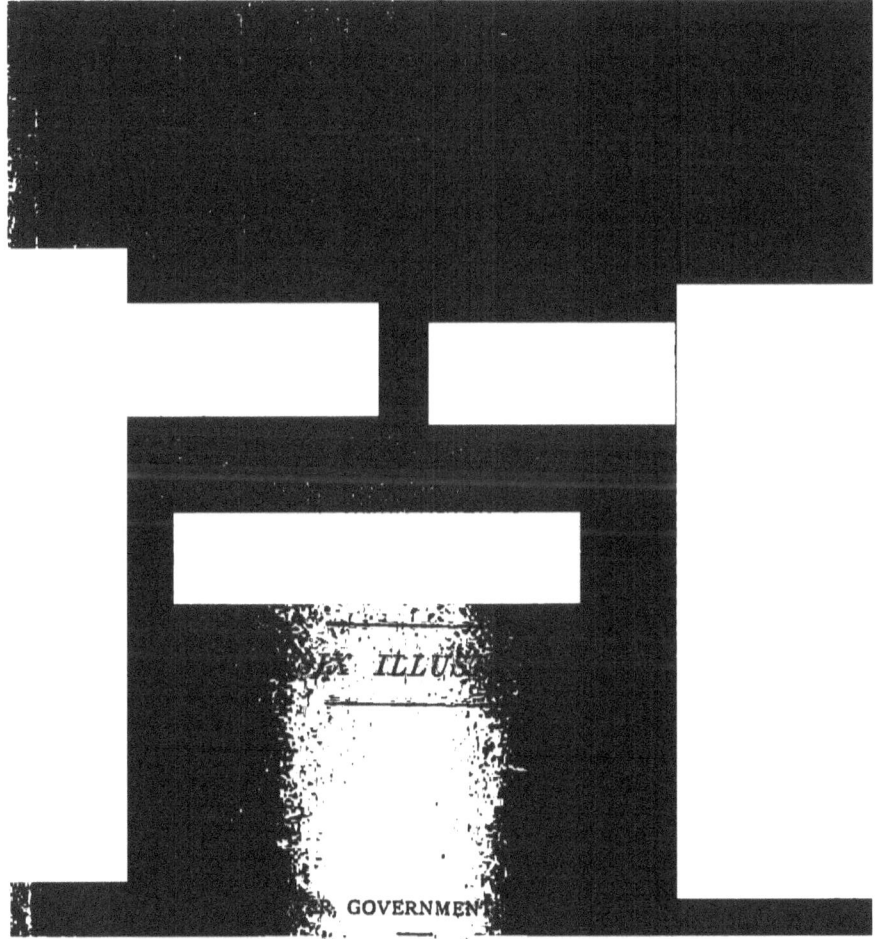

EX ILLUS

GOVERNMENT

1896.
[2s.]

INTRODUCTORY.

THESE notes on " Gems and Precious Stones " originally appeared in the " New South Wales Educational Gazette," at intervals from August, 1892, to May, 1894.

They were primarily intended for the use of our Public School Teachers, whose stations are, of course, as widespread as the Colony itself, in the hope that they might form the basis of object lessons, and also lead, perhaps, to discoveries of precious stones.

So extensive has been the correspondence which has resulted from these articles (some long out of print), that a few months ago I requested Mr. Smith to prepare them for publication in a separate form. This he has done, at the same time bringing the information up to date, and supplementing it where it was considered desirable to do so.

J. H. MAIDEN.

PREFACE.

IN the preparation of the following notes on "Gems and Precious Stones" for re-publication, in a form more suited to the requirements of the general public, it has been recognised that many who feel an interest in these useful and valuable minerals may have had but little scientific training, and whose knowledge of gems only extends to those cut and polished specimens used in articles of adornment. The endeavour has, therefore, been made to simplify the information, by ignoring scientific expressions and highly technical terms as much as possible, but where the use of these was unavoidable, explanatory notes have been added to elucidate their meaning.

It may be well to mention that the natural minerals have but little resemblance to the finished gems as prepared for sale, and while an attempt has been made to convey the meaning and appearance of simple crystalline forms in the four principal systems, it must be understood that it is seldom that the natural crystals are perfect in form, or regular in appearance. This might tend to mislead one little acquainted with the laws that govern form in minerals, although a little consideration would enable one to place a crystallized specimen in its proper system ; the diamond, the zircon, and the sapphire for instance, could not be mistaken for each other when found crystallized, although, perhaps, identical in colour. In water-worn specimens, of course, other tests have to be applied, these are fully described in the following pages, and the differences pointed out between gems resembling each other in some respects. The methods adopted in determining the physical properties of minerals are also fully explained.

It has been attempted, by introducing well authenticated historical facts, to enliven an otherwise rather dry subject with interesting narrative, much of which has been obtained from the information collected and published by Messrs. Streeter, Emanuel, King, Dieulafait, Kunz, Burnham, and others. To the authors of these works my obligations are due. While endeavouring to make the information of some educational value, it must be understood that no attempt has been made to write for those who are already scientifically acquainted with the subject, as they are well provided for by very many works of reference.

Technological Museum,
    Sydney, New South Wales,
       January, 1896.

CONTENTS.

GEMS AND PRECIOUS STONES,

WITH

DESCRIPTIONS OF THEIR DISTINCTIVE PROPERTIES; THE METHODS FOR DETERMINING THEM, &c.

General Remarks.

THE collection of gems and precious stones in the Technological Museum forms the basis of the following inquiries and investigations, with special reference to the gems of New South Wales. In speaking of precious stones, great latitude must be allowed, because it is not easy to define in a sentence what we mean by the term. The line of demarcation between stones that are precious and those not so considered is very narrow; but there are certain points, however, that cannot be overlooked. First they must be rare, then they must be beautiful, and of course without the property of durability they would be of little value. Certain minerals contain these properties in a very high degree, and have consequently been held in great esteem from the earliest times.

.The occupation of searching for precious stones is useful and often lucrative, and in a country so rich in mineral wealth as New South Wales, the prospect of succeeding in the search is a reasonable one.

It is intended to deal with the subject in such a plain and simple manner that those who know little of the subject of mineralogy may be enabled to discriminate between the stones. Of course it is not to be supposed that anyone will be made an expert by perusing this work, but the information here given will prevent one going to a lot of useless trouble over worthless specimens.

For a full investigation it would be well to forward a sample of a supposed gem to the Technological Museum, and any communication addressed to the Curator of that Institution will receive every consideration. It is desirable that those who correspond with the Museum should give information as to the localities where the specimens were found, their matrix, and if possible the geological formation from which they were obtained.

A small amount of knowledge as to the methods of testing minerals, especially their specific gravity, hardness, and mode of crystallization, would often save a great deal of annoyance and prevent disappointment, because it is a common occurrence to find a collection consisting of little else than varieties of quartz, with perhaps a garnet or two.

A

When we consider the enormous quantity of diamonds that have been recovered from the mines of South Africa, of Brazil, and of India, we must acknowledge that up to the present time very little has been accomplished in the Australian Colonies in this industry.

Diamonds were known to exist in New South Wales as early as 1859*, in fact before their rediscovery in South Africa, and yet, in comparison, virtually nothing has been done here. Every field had a beginning, and since diamonds are known to exist in different localities in this Colony, it remains for someone to succeed in locating their position in payable quantities, which result will no doubt eventually be brought about by systematic search or by accident.

Although the diamond fields of such marvellous richness were often discovered in a very simple manner, yet, we find that those who were the fortunate ones, usually had some knowledge of these gems to guide them, either from the appearance of the stones themselves, or of the geological similarities. Although in most things the proverb is correct, " that a little knowledge is a dangerous thing," yet, in the discovery of diamond fields, it evidently does not apply. It is reported that in 1754 a slave, who had been transported from the province of Minas Geraes, Brazil, to Bahia in the same country, discovered diamonds in the latter place, because of the similarity of soil and geological formation between the two districts, thus succeeding in opening up one of the richest fields for diamonds ever discovered.†

The Sincora Mine in the Province of Bahia, was discovered about the year 1843, by a mulatto miner, who had previously been engaged in washing for diamonds. He went by himself searching for these gems, and laboured successfully for some days, till want of provisions drove him home. He returned with the stones he had collected, which he offered for sale to some of the people engaged at another mine. As the stones were of different quality, it was suggested that he had discovered another mine. He denied having done so, and was thrown into prison, accused of having stolen the diamonds ; he at last confessed to his discovery and was released. In about eight months nearly 15,000 persons arrived at the place, and the diamonds were found in such quantity, that in two years it is surmised that nearly 600,000 carats were obtained and forwarded to Europe. The value of the diamonds exported from this field must certainly have been very great. The enormous numbers of diamonds that have been found in South Africa has done much to reduce the importance of the Brazilian fields, as previously these Brazilian mines had reduced the importance of those of India.

The South African diamond-fields are situated north of the Orange River, in the province of Griqualand West, at a distance of about 500 miles from the coast.

The story of the discovery (or rather re-discovery, for, although unknown to Europeans until that time, the natives had for many years been aware of their existence), is that a trader named John O'Reilly was, in the year 1867, travelling southward from the Orange River, when he rested his team

---

* " *Researches in the Southern Gold Fields.*" Rev. W. B. Clarke, M.A. Page 272.

† We have an analogous case in the history of mining in New South Wales. I allude to the discovery of gold in this Colony by Mr. Hargreaves, who, gaining his knowledge in California, came all the way to the place in this Colony he knew so well, to search for gold, because of the geological resemblance between the two places.

at a farm for the night. The owner of the farm showed him some stones, among which he found a diamond. From a letter addressed to the Governor of Cape Colony (Sir Henry Barkly) by Mr. O'Reilly, some five years after the first discovery, we learn :—

"In March, 1867, I was on my way to Colesberg from the junction of the Vaal and Orange Rivers. I outspanned at Mr. Niekerk's farm, when I saw a beautiful lot of Orange River stones on his table, and which I examined. I told Niekerk they were very pretty. He showed me another lot, out of which I at once picked the first diamond. I asked him for it, and he told me I could have it, as it belonged to a bushman boy of Daniel Jacobs. I took it at once to Hope Town, and made Mr. Chalmers, Civil Commissioner, aware of the discovery. I then took it on to Colesberg and gave it to the Acting Civil Commissioner there for transmission to Cape Town to the High Commissioner. The Acting Civil Commissioner sent it to Dr. Atherstone, of Graham's Town, who forwarded it to Cape Town."

Dr. Atherstone wrote that the specimen was a veritable diamond, weighing $21\frac{1}{4}$ carats, and that it was worth £500, and also that from where it came there must be lots more.

Although returning at once to the locality where it was obtained, he was not at all successful in searching for other specimens, and it was not until 1869 that Van Niekerk secured from a Griqua or Hottentot, a large stone, for which he gave the sum of £400 or live stock to that value. He sold it at once to Messrs. Lilienfeld, of Hope Town, for over £10,000. This was the famous "Star of South Africa." It weighed, $83\frac{1}{2}$ carats in the rough, and was estimated to be worth £25,000.

How many of the settlers in the interior of this and the other colonies have had at one time or another a prize in their possession (not, perhaps, as valuable as the diamond referred to) and have not known it? In the early days of the Mudgee fields, diamonds were cast on one side undiscovered, gold being then sought for. I would impress on anyone finding or collecting a peculiar stone the importance of ascertaining what it really is.

The Gani Mine, or "Gani Coulour," described by Tavernier, and at his time employing 60,000 persons, was situated in the celebrated province of Golconda, in South Central India. It was accidentally discovered by a native labourer whilst digging a piece of ground for agricultural purposes, his first important find being a stone of 25 carats. A very large number of diamonds were soon obtained, some of large size. The "Great Mogul" was obtained here, an immense diamond weighing $787\frac{1}{2}$ carats as the lowest estimation; it was of the first water and valued at an enormous amount.

As will be seen, when we come to deal with the geological formation of the diamondiferous strata of the various countries where diamonds are found in any quantity, the conditions of occurrence are not the same in different countries, so that we can hardly judge by analogy where to look or what part to prospect; the only thing that we can do is to obtain as much benefit from previous experience as possible. There appears to be no definite reason why mining for diamonds, and other precious stones, should not be an industry of the greatest importance in this Colony, and confer the same benefits on New South Wales as it has done in Africa, Brazil, and other countries.

It will be better, perhaps, before proceeding to give an account of the individual gem-stones, to describe the methods adopted in their discrimination. It is evident that methods have to be taken to arrive at this result without destroying the specimen, and it is by taking advantage of the physical properties of the stones themselves, that we are enabled to decide what the specimen is that is under investigation.

Physical Properties of Minerals.

In the determination of this class of minerals, the greatest advantage is taken of their optical and other physical characters, and in nearly all cases these are sufficient to enable one to arrive at a decision as to the correct name of a specimen.

The most important of these characters is the crystalline form, and in many instances this alone is sufficient to determine the supposed gem. It will be convenient to defer consideration of the several systems of crystallization until dealing with a typical gem, as the cubical with the diamond, the hexagonal with the ruby, and so on through the different systems.

The other characters necessary to be understood are the following :—

Hardness.	Electricity.	Lustre.
Specific gravity.	Cleavage.	Pleochroism.

Hardness.

The scientific definition of hardness, is the resistance one substance offers to the mechanical pressure of another. It is one of the most important tests, in fact, the first that should be used when determining a mineral. But a mistake must not be made in arriving at a decision too soon; because, when attempting to scratch one mineral with another, a mark often appears to be left upon the stone *tested*, but which is only a portion of the abraded surface of the stone *testing*, and this apparent scratch may be easily removed with the finger.

The scale in general use is that known as Mohs', and is as follows :—

1. Talc.
2. Gypsum.
3. Calcite (the transparent variety).
4. Fluor Spar (crystallized).
5. Apatite.
6. Felspar (Orthoclase).
7. Quartz.
8. Topaz.
9. Sapphire or Corundum.
10. Diamond.

Nos. 6, 7, 8, and 9 are obtainable without much difficulty, and should be kept for easy reference.

A penknife of the very best quality will hardly scratch more than 6, and it is advisable to consider that when a mineral is scratched by a penknife its hardness will be between 5 and 6.

Window glass will replace apatite on an emergency.

When testing the hardness of a mineral the attempt should be made upon similar parts of crystals, and upon unweathered surfaces. If a stone will scratch quartz, but is itself scratched by topaz, its hardness is between 7 and 8, a little judgment being necessary to decide whether this is nearer 7 than 8.

It is not advisable to attempt to scratch a cut and polished specimen upon a prominent face, but, if unmounted, the "girdle" may be used for the test. The recognised hardness of each gem-stone will be given when describing the individual stones.

As it is sometimes difficult to obtain some of the minerals enumerated above, the following list may be used instead:—

1. May be impressed with the finger nail.
2. Does not scratch a plate of copper.
3. Scratches copper, but is also scratched by it.
4. Is not scratched by copper, but does not scratch glass.
5. Scratches glass slightly ; is scratched with a knife.
6. Scratches glass easily ; is scarcely scratched with a good knife.
7. Is not scratched with a knife, but just yields to a file.
8. Cannot be filed, but scratches a rock crystal.
9. Scratches a topaz.
10. Scratches a ruby or sapphire.

As illustrating the importance of hardness in precious stones, the following is instructive : In the Brazilian mines a negro of Villa do Principe informed the Prince Regent that he was in possession of a very large diamond, and that he wished to present it to His Royal Highness. An escort was sent to bring the diamond, together with its owner, to the capital, a journey which occupied twenty-eight days. When the specimen arrived, it was of such a large size that it was thought hardly possible that so enormous a diamond could exist, its weight being nearly one pound. It was, however, sent to the treasury under a strong guard. When the simple test of scratching with a real diamond was applied it was found to be readily scratched, and much to the disappointment of all concerned it was found to be rock-crystal or quartz. The test of hardness is one so easily applied, that it is inexcusable that anyone should be deceived between these two minerals.

Specific Gravity.

This is an invaluable assistance in the determination of precious stones. The term is used to express the weight of a substance as compared with some other substance, water being the standard of comparison for minerals ; the temperature of the water being taken at 60 deg. Fahrenheit or $15\cdot5$ deg. centigrade. It is better to use the water the correct temperature, to do away with the necessity for correction.

Having obtained the weight of the mineral by careful weighing in air, it is suspended or placed in water and again weighed, the difference being the weight of water equal in size to the specimen. Divide the weight in air by the loss of weight in water, and the quotient will be the specific gravity.

A stone weighs in air	...	...	...	32·6 grains.
„ in water	...	...	...	20·1 „
Loss of weight in water	...	...	...	12·5 „

Dividing the weight in air by the loss of weight in water, we get 2·6 as the specific gravity of the stone, near enough for practical purposes.

On the fact that a solid, when immersed in a fluid, loses a portion of its weight, and that this portion is equal to the weight of the fluid which it displaces, that is, to the weight of its own bulk of that fluid, is based the well-known theorem of Archimedes.

To obtain the exact weight of that fluid displaced is the only difficulty. Fair sized specimens may be suspended directly from a balance into water, and the difference in that fluid from that in air thus obtained, but for small specimens, or where great accuracy is required, this mode of arriving at the loss of weight is not sufficiently delicate, without a very delicate balance is in the possession of the operator. The mode of obtaining the specific gravity is perhaps best performed with a specific-gravity bottle; this is a small bottle with a small well-fitting stopper, and usually having a hole bored through the glass stopper, to allow most accurate filling, and to prevent air bubbles. The bottle is first weighed full of water of the standard temperature, and carefully dried; the weight of the specimen in air is next determined, its weight noted, and added to that of the bottle filled with water; the solid is then put into the bottle, displacing of course an equal bulk of water, the weight of which is determined by the loss on again weighing; the weight of the water displaced is then divided into the weight of the solid, and the answer is the specific gravity.

Example—

Glass bottle filled with water	...	...	294·69	grains.
Weight of stone in air ...	...	...	8·18	,,
			302·87	,,
After displacing the water by the stone, the weight was ...	...	...	300·17	,,
Displaced water weighed ...	...	2·70	,,
Specific gravity $\dfrac{8·18}{2·7}$	...	...	3·03	,,

A small glass phial, with small glass stopper ground into it, and a notch filed the length of the stopper will answer fairly well; or an ordinary stopper will do, if the neck of the bottle is filled entirely, and the stopper slid into its place over the edge to prevent air bubbles, always inserting the stopper in exactly the same position. The author has made some very satisfactory determinations with a bottle of this character, comparing results with a first-class specific gravity bottle. There are other methods which are often used for this purpose, such as the use of alcohol instead of water to overcome the great friction between the gem and the water; then corrections have often to be made for temperature, &c., but it will be hardly necessary to describe them fully here.

Solutions of known density are sometimes used for obtaining the specific gravity value of gems, but these are somewhat difficult of manipulation.

Determination of specific gravity affords in many instances a test of the greatest value, and prevents the possibility in most cases of substituting one gem for another, such as white topaz or white sapphire for the diamond; moreover, it is a test easily applied, and there is no fear of injuring the gems in the slightest degree.

It is immaterial what system of weights is used.

The following determinations were made by the author, to decide the identity of a few small red stones from the Cudgegong River, near Mudgee, in this Colony, and are here given as illustrating the advantage of the specific gravity method to confirm other tests. The specimens were of a ruby colour, rather flat water-worn particles, and free from any sign of crystalline form. Although minute, it was considered that they scratched topaz. This test, if entirely satisfactory, would be sufficient to suggest that they were rubies, but confirmatory tests are required for scientific classification.

With the dichroiscope they gave squares of different colours, both reddish and well marked. This indicated the ruby, and proved them not to be garnets or spinels.

They were infusible, but reverted to their original colour on cooling; this colour test indicated that they were not zircons.

The specific gravity was taken, using a delicate assay balance, and diluted alcohol as the liquid, suspending the stones in a platinum wire cage directly into the alcohol, which had a specific gravity of ·872 when cooled to the normal temperature. The following results were obtained, using the metric system of weights :—

Weight of gems in air =...   ...   ...   ·2947 gram.
     „   „   alcohol = ...   ·2300   „

Loss of weight in alcohol = ...   ·0647   „

$$\therefore \quad \frac{·2947 \times ·872}{·0647} = 3·9718 \text{ as specific gravity.}$$

By using a small specific-gravity bottle with distilled water at the normal temperature, and the whole of the gems, the following figures were obtained:—

Weight of gems in air = ...   ·6968 gram.
     „   bottle + water = ...   36·6320   „

                                              37·3288   „
     „   bottle + water + gems = ...   37·1534   „

Displaced water weighs = ...   ·1754   „

$$\therefore \quad \frac{·6968}{·1754} = 3·9726 \text{ as specific gravity, almost identical with the above.}$$

From these results we are justified in considering these gems as rubies, and they have been placed in the collection named as such.

In the Russian Court at the London Exhibition of 1851 there was a beautiful stone labelled Phenacite, which is a silicate of glucina, and it is used in Russia as a gem-stone. Experts' opinions differed as to whether this was the correct name for the specimen. The owner's permission was obtained, and the stone tested. On taking the specific gravity it was found to be 3·5. The specific gravity of phenacite being at the highest 3, it was at once proved not to be that mineral, and on further tests being applied it was found to be a topaz.

Electricity.

As a large number of gems develop this property more or less, it is of some importance in their discrimination.

Friction will develop electricity in the diamond and topaz most markedly. The diamond displays positive electricity whether it be polished or in its rough state. Other gems are positively electric in the polished state only, and only have the power of developing negative electricity when in their rough state.

This development of electricity in a mineral may be seen by its power of attracting or repelling a light pith pellet suspended by cotton, or better, by a silken cord from a glass rod; or a small piece of cotton wool suspended in the same manner will answer the purpose; even a piece of paper will be attracted in this way.

Pyro-electricity, or that developed by heat, is very marked in some minerals ; tourmaline especially, when heated to not more than 150° C., and suspended by a silken thread, will behave like an electro-magnet, having positive and negative poles.   Pyro-electricity is mostly developed by those minerals whose crystals are terminated by different crystalline faces at the different ends, and which are called from this peculiarity hemimorphic.

Besides tourmaline, topaz and axinite afford examples of pyro-electricity. Very great care must be taken in heating stones by fire, because in some cases where cleavage is very perfect they might split, as in topaz, which has a very perfect cleavage.

An easy method of distinguishing between green tourmaline and olivine is by heating, the former developing pyro-electricity while the latter does not.

Cleavage.

This is the property possessed by many minerals of splitting in certain directions more readily than in others ; in each cleavable mineral bearing a constant relation to a certain face, or to certain faces, of the form in which the mineral crystallizes.   Minerals may cleave in one or more directions, but one cleavage is generally to be obtained with greater ease than the others. Topaz has a very perfect basal cleavage—that is, parallel to the base of the prism, or at right angles to the longer axis, and in rolled stones a portion of a smooth cleaved face is often found on topaz. Beryl also has a basal cleavage, although somewhat indistinct. There is also a basal cleavage in corundum and its varieties, which is sometimes perfect. The diamond has a perfect cleavage, parallel to the faces of the octahedron, this being the primary form of the cubical system, to which the diamond belongs. Cleavages are known as *perfect*, when smooth and readily obtained, or *imperfect*, when obtained with difficulty. The latter are not so smooth.

The diamond cutter avails himself of this natural property of this gem to remove damaged portions, &c.   Dr. Wollaston, in the early part of this century, was one of the first to call attention to the advantages offered by the ready cleavage of the diamond.   He purchased a rough, badly-flawed stone from a firm who considered it too bad to pay for the cutting; then, removing the defective parts by cleavage, he had the perfect portion cut, and resold the cut stone to the firm from whom he first bought it, at a very large profit.

But the cleavage of the diamond must have been known long before this period, because Dr. Boot, writing in 1609, tells us that he knew a physician who boasted that he could divide a diamond into small scales like a piece of talc.   The flat gems of Indian origin also point to the fact that the cleavage of the diamond was well known.

In early times an idea existed that owing to the extraordinary hardness of the diamond it could not be broken by a hammer on an anvil; but this was erroneous, because a diamond can be reduced to grains by a heavy pestle and mortar, on account of its perfect cleavage.   This will, perhaps, account for the fact that the ancients had no knowledge of great diamonds, as they placed them upon the anvil to test their genuineness.

This supposed property of the diamond of resisting the blow of a hammer is mentioned both by Lucretius and Pliny.   The latter says that the test of all these diamonds is made upon an anvil by blows of the hammer, and their repulsion from iron is such that they make the hammer fly to pieces, and sometimes the anvil is broken.   This error was not eradicated until comparatively modern times, for in 1476, when after the battle of Morat, the Swiss soldiers seized upon the tent of Charles the Bold, they found in it, among other treasures, a certain number of diamonds, and in order to test whether they were genuine, struck them with hammers and hatchets, and of course broke many of them to pieces.

Lustre.

This term is applied to the reflection of light from the surfaces of the specimens; it is influenced by the nature of those surfaces, some reflecting more light than others.

There are six forms of lustre which may be applied to precious stones, as follows:—

Adamantine	...	The well-known lustre of the diamond.
Resinous	...	The lustre of the garnet.
Vitreous	...	That of the emerald.
Waxy ...	...	Resembling turquoise.
Pearly ...	...	Shown in moonstone.
Silky ...	...	Like crocidolite.

Each of the above varieties of lustre may differ in intensity, but the different forms of these are more marked in minerals other than gems.

The several other properties of light, as refraction, dispersion, polarisation, and pleochroism act in different ways with different stones, but it will be unnecessary to notice them with the exception of the last.

Pleochroism.

Means the condition of displaying many colours; a stone is dichroic when it exhibits two colours; trichroic when it shows three, which is the highest grade of pleochroism. This property, well marked in precious stones, is a useful one, and easy of determination; a little instrument, called a dichroiscope, is used in this investigation. It consists of a short tube, in which is placed a prism of Iceland spar; at one end, farthest from the eye, a little square hole is placed, at the other a small lens. With this little instrument the dichroism of a large majority of gems may be discovered, provided they are coloured. Holding the stone before the little square hole, and looking through the tube towards the light, two squares will be seen, and if the stone is dichroic these squares will be of different colours. A ruby will show two reds of different hues, while the garnet will give the same hue to both squares, and the difference between the ruby and the spinel is at once seen in the same manner. Besides the ruby; the sapphire, tourmaline, emerald, topaz, aquamarine, beryl, chrysoberyl, iolite, and amethyst, all show squares of different colours, and are thus easily determined from their imitations.

The remaining physical properties of minerals are, in the study of gems, of little moment, and will not be considered here.

Individual gems will now be described in detail, commencing, of course, with the most important of them all.

DIAMOND.

Crystalline system=cubic.
Hardness=10.
Specific gravity=3·52.
Lustre=Adamantine.
Cleavage=Parallel to faces of the octahedron, highly perfect.
Composition=Carbon, being chemically the same as graphite (black lead) and charcoal. Although so different in appearance, in hardness, and in specific gravity, from the other forms under which carbon is known, yet, when analysed, they are found to be identical. The diamond may be considered as the crystallized form of carbon, while charcoal and lamp black are amorphous.

The crystalline form of minerals is of the greatest importance, and is of special value in the determination of gems ; it indicates the difference between substances in many respects resembling each other.

Through ignorance of the crystalline form of the diamond, a gentleman in California once offered £200 for a small specimen of quartz. He knew nothing about gems; but this being a bright shining substance, not scratched by the file used, but sufficiently hard to scratch glass, he considered that these qualities belonged only to the diamond, and offered what he thought a fair price for the specimen. The owner's knowledge was no better, as he refused the offer.

It is a common mistake to suppose that if a stone will scratch glass, and is bright and glistening, that it must be a diamond. Natural quartz crystals are often more brilliant than those of the diamond when in its rough state, and being sometimes very minute, with a very bright lustre, these little worthless stones might easily deceive one; but the crystalline form and the hardness are generally sufficient to determine them. The diamond, in its natural state, is often deficient of that lustre one expects in this gem, and for that reason is often, no doubt, overlooked by miners and others searching for gold in Australia. An octahedron crystal in the Museum collection is very deficient in lustre, and might easily be missed when with other white stones, although its crystalline form should cause detection at once.

By its crystalline form alone it is easy to distinguish the diamond from those minerals that somewhat resemble it in colour and lustre; from quartz, this crystallizing in the hexagonal system; from white zircon, belonging to the tetragonal system; from topaz, which is rhombic; from white sapphire, or colourless corundum, which is hexagonal. But while the crystalline forms are so important, the extreme hardness of the diamond is characteristic, it being able to scratch all other known substances. This test of hardness is of the greatest importance, especially when dealing with gem-stones with crystalline forms obscured.

The specific gravity of quartz being at the most 2·8, would readily determine the difference between it and the diamond, while zircon has a specific gravity as high as 4·7. Topaz, having nearly the same specific gravity as the diamond, is easily distinguished by its deficient hardness and other physical properties.

When the diamond is rubbed it exhibits positive electricity.

Ordinary solvents have not the slightest effect on the diamond.

Colour.

By far the larger number of diamonds are colourless, or nearly so, but specimens of nearly all colours have been obtained.

Black diamonds of great beauty are occasionally obtained in Borneo. These are extra hard, the ordinary diamond dust making little impression upon them, their own dust having to be used for the purpose of cutting and polishing them. A black diamond weighing 350 carats was exhibited at the London Exhibition in 1851, and was greatly admired. A short time ago Mr. Streeter had on exhibition at the Imperial Institute, London, a black diamond.

Blue diamonds are seldom found, but when of a deep blue colour and perfect in other respects they are very valuable. The celebrated " Hope " diamond, weighing 44¼ carats, is a beautiful blue, and a very valuable stone. A model of this gem is in the Museum collection. (*See Notes on historical diamonds at page* 17.)

Red diamonds are rare, and when good are of great value.

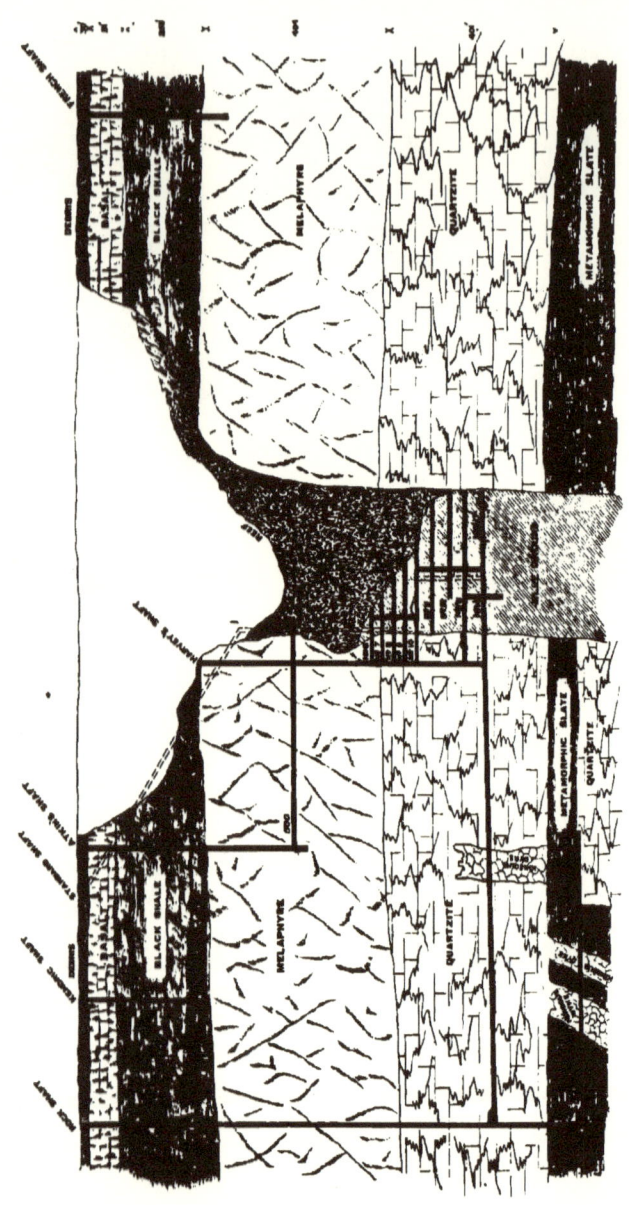

Green diamonds of good colour are also rare and valuable, a specimen at Dresden weighing 48⅓ carats being valued at £30,000.

In the celebrated Townshend collection are included diamonds having black, yellow, green, grey, indigo, cinnamon, and other colours. This collection was presented by the Rev. Chauncy Hare Townshend, in 1869, to the South Kensington Museum, and contains 154 specimens.

"Bort," or "Boort," is a name given to an uncrystallized form of diamond. It is crushed to form "diamond dust" for polishing purposes. It may be as well to mention here that those diamonds that are too bad for cutting as gems are known as "bort," and are crushed for polishing and cutting purposes. It has been stated that a specimen of "bort" was obtained near Bathurst. It would certainly be advisable to keep this substance in mind when seeking for gems.

"Carbonado" is an opaque, very hard form of carbon—as hard as the diamond. It is only found in Brazil at present. It is used for polishing, and for the manufacture of "diamond drills" for deep borings. The demand for it for these purposes has increased its value, it being worth at one time 30s. per carat.

Geological Formation.

In New South Wales, diamonds are principally obtained from the tertiary gravels and recent drifts; but it is hardly to be supposed that they were formed in these tertiary deposits. They, no doubt, originally had a home in some older formation, and it certainly is desirable that this secret dwelling-place should be discovered. This may probably be metamorphosed rocks.

Under what conditions diamonds have been formed is at present unknown, so that we cannot presume to suggest the kind of formation most likely to contain them. The operation of excessive heat in their formation seems hardly probable, on account of the combustible nature of the diamond. Whether the carbon was derived from animal, vegetable, or other sources, is also unknown, but the presence of the diamond in mica-slate does not favour the idea of vegetable origin.

There is not the smallest doubt that the enormous yield of diamonds from the "Kimberley diggings" of South Africa, is due to the fact that there the diamond is taken from its actual matrix, where it is found in an intrusive rock. In this rock the diamonds are found crystallized, often in octahedrons and allied forms. The formation in which these diamonds are found is a very peculiar one, consisting, as it does, of material filling a natural "pipe," with hard rock around it. The generally accepted theory is that the "pipe" is the funnel of an extinct volcano, and that the diamond-bearing rock which now fills it, and forms the mine, has been upheaved from a vast depth, the diamonds being probably of earlier date than the upheaval.

By referring to the accompanying diagram, a good idea will be obtained of this peculiar occurrence. It is from an official publication issued by the Government of Cape Colony (Report of the Inspector of Diamond Mines, Kimberley, for 1892). Although indicating the Kimberley Mine, the general idea will serve for the other principal mines also.

The inevitable rush to this district set in during 1870, and it is computed that in a short time no less than 10,000 persons were searching for diamonds there. Since that time the diamond-fields of South Africa have become noted for their marvellous richness, diamonds by the ton weight having been found there. For a little over three years—1883, 1884, 1885, and part of 1882—diamonds to the value of over £8,250,000 sterling were obtained. The value of the rough stones ranged during that time between 20s. and 29s. per carat.

The majority of these diamonds were obtained from the four principal mines, viz., the Kimberley, De Beer's, Bultfontein, and Du Toit's Pan.

It is computed that up to the end of 1885 no less than 6¼ tons weight of diamonds had been obtained from these four mines, realising no less than £40,000,000 sterling.

Since that time the yield has gone on increasing, for, taking the five years from 1888 to 1892 inclusive, we find that the amount of carats of diamonds exported from Cape Colony was 15,603,248 valued at £20,590,726, or about £1 6s. 5d. per carat.

Besides these deposits where the diamonds are obtained by systematic mining, there are many diamonds found in the river deposits also, particularly on the banks of the Vaal River, from its junction with the Orange to above Christiana. The "diggings" are between these two points, and on both banks of the Vaal River, a distance of about 70 miles. The amount of diamonds obtained from these river "diggings" is not an insignificant item; it is computed that the value of the stones that have been here obtained must be between £2,000,000 and £3,000,000 sterling.

The original home of these diamonds is still subject to controversy, but they are all found in alluvial soil in a deposit of ferruginous gravel, mixed with red sand, lime, and boulders.

In Brazil the diamonds are found in a group of rocks called the Itacolumite series, because a peculiar form of sandstone called Itacolumite occurs there. In thin pieces portions of this sandstone are flexible, and can be bent backward and forward without breaking. This form of sandstone is associated with a group of schists containing specular iron ore. Traversing these rocks are certain veins of clayey material containing diamonds. In the quartzites of an overlying series diamonds are also found. Probably the lower metamorphic series was the original home of the diamond in this locality.

It is stated that in Borneo the diamond has been found in serpentine, although they are generally obtained from the diamondiferous gravels in the neighbourhood of Martapura.

In Borneo the diamond is usually associated with gold, platinum, and gem stones.

There appears to be little doubt but that the earliest known diamonds came from India, and it is almost certain that down to comparatively modern times no other locality was known where diamonds were obtained in any quantity. Although obtained at one time in large quantities, the yield of diamonds from the fields now worked is small. The export trade is of little importance, the industry having been virtually destroyed by the vast quantities of diamonds obtained in Brazil during the last century, and in South Africa during the last thirty years. The Indian mines were originally spread over a large portion of the country, extending from near the River Ganges, in Bundelcund, to the Pennaur River in the Madras Presidency. The diamonds are generally found in superficial and alluvial deposits of comparatively recent formation, although they have been stated to be found *in situ* in the ancient rocks of the great Vindhyan formation. From the evidence obtained of the formations where the diamond is found, it is to be supposed that they have originally been derived from the disintregation of rocks belonging to the older geological systems.

Previous to the year 1889 about 50,000 diamonds had been found in New South Wales at the several localities named below, the largest weighing 16·2 grains or about 5¾ carats. For two or three years after this date searching for diamonds does not appear to have been a very lucrative occupation, but not long since the industry was reviving at Bingera, and much interest was taken in some very successful washings that took place there.

At Bingera the diamonds are found in a conglomerate or "wash" as it is termed, and at the principal mine at a depth of 50 to 60 feet, but both the drift and the thickness of the diamondiferous portion are, as far as opened out, found to be very irregularly deposited. The diamonds are usually small and a great many are "off colour," but appear to be plentifully distributed in portions of the conglomerate. Captain Rogers has done much pioneer work in the district, working alone against all difficulties, and at one time his mine, the Monte Christo, caused some excitement in mining circles, as a good many diamonds were obtained from the "wash" taken from the mine. Several other individuals and companies have also at various times prospected this district, with occasionally a fair amount of success, but during 1894 the whole of the diamond mining companies obtained suspension of the labour conditions.* It is certainly not too much to expect that at some future date mining for diamonds will be a successful industry at this locality or neighbourhood, and perhaps reach gigantic proportions. We must not forget the unfavourable report of an expert who reported on the diamond fields of South Africa before they became an accomplished fact. The following extract is sufficient :—"From the geological character of the district, which he had very carefully and thoroughly examined, it was *impossible* that diamonds had been or could ever be found there."

When the diamond fields of Brazil were first established, attempts were made to depreciate the diamonds because of prevailing interests. It is hardly to be expected that assistance will be forthcoming to prospect the diamondiferous districts of this Colony from those who are interested in existing mines or existing stocks. Although the deposits at present known may not be remunerative, still there probably exists other deposits in the neighbourhood, not yet known, that will be found to be so.

As already stated, it was Rev. W. B. Clarke, M.A., who drew attention to the presence of diamonds in the Colony, and mentioned a few localities where they had been found. That some interest was taken, even at that time, in this matter may be gathered from a statement made by that gentleman, that several people had forwarded to him specimens of rock crystal (quartz), of topaz, and of white zircon, under the impression that they were diamonds.

The principal minerals usually found with diamonds in New South Wales are gold, ruby, sapphire, zircon, garnet, topaz, tourmaline, ilmenite, magnetite, corundum, and quartz.

Diamonds should be sought for in all auriferous drifts.

---

* A recent report on the Bingera Diamond Fields, by G. A. Stonier, F.G S., is published in the Annual Report of the Department of Mines, N.S.W., for the year 1894.

Localities, N.S.W.

The following list of localities where the diamond has been already found in the Colony, may be of use to enable one to see what parts are at present known to be diamondiferous; they are principally taken from Professor Liversidge's excellent work " Minerals of New South Wales."

County Bathurst.—Bathurst District, Reedy Creek.
,,   Bland.—Calabash Creek.
,,   Bligh.—Cudgegong River.
,,   Buller.—Ruby tin-mine.
,,   Camden.—Mittagong.
,,   Georgiana.—Trunkey.
,,   Gough.—Britannia Mine, Inverell, Middle Creek, Newstead, Stannifer, Vegetable Creek (Emmaville), and several creeks in this district.
,,   Hardinge.—Auburn Vale Creek, Bengonover Mine, Big River, Borah Mine, Cope's Creek.
,,   Murchison.—Bingera, Doctor's Creek.
,,   Phillip.—Cudgegong River, near Mudgee.
,,   Rous.—Near Ballina.
,,   Roxburgh.—Turon River.
,,   Sandon.—Uralla.
,,   St. Vincent.—Shoalhaven River.
,,   Wellington.—Bald Hills, Burrandong, Monkey Hill, Pyramul Creek, Sally's Flat, Two-mile Flat.
,,   Westmoreland.—Oberon.

Following these localities on a geological map of New South Wales, we find that, considered broadly, the diamond is found in the older geological formations, and also that there exists in this portion of the Colony a predominance of plutonic and igneous rocks; that this stretch of country extends outside the permo-carboniferous area, from the County St. Vincent in the south, to County Buller, in the north, and embraces the country where gold and tin are principally distributed.

The diamond fields, near Mudgee, on the Cudgegong River, at one time worked, have somewhat similar geological characteristics to those existing at Bingera. The diamonds at the former locality were found in a conglomerate capped by basalt, and the associated minerals were almost identical with those found with the diamonds at Bingera. In the Museum collection are two fine octahedron crystals from near Mudgee.

During the year 1894 search was again made in the Mittagong district for payable diamondiferous drift, but without success.

Composition of the Diamond.

It is only in comparatively recent times that the composition of the diamond has been known. Newton judged from its very high refractive power that it would eventually be found to be combustible.

Boyle appears to be the first who by experiment proved that its nature was different from the generality of stones. He showed that under the influence of great heat the diamond disappeared. At frequent intervals after this experiment many others were carried out, demonstrating the fact that at any rate the diamond could be made to disappear when burned in air; but it remained for the renowned Davy to solve the problem by analysing the diamond and thus proving its composition. When thus analysed the diamond

CUBICAL SYSTEM.
Simple forms.

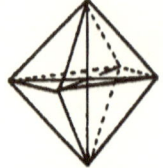

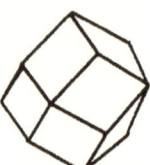

Octahedron.   *Cube.*   *Rhombic Dodecahedron.*

Triakis Octahedron.   *Hexakis Octahedron.*   *Icositetrahedron.*

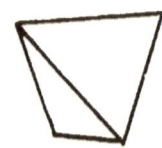

Tetrahedron.   *Hexakis Tetrahedron.*   *Combination of 1. 2 and 3.*

(5 a 201-95-6.)

was found to be composed of carbon, with a trace of metallic impurity.   It may seem remarkable that such a beautiful object should be composed of such common material as carbon, but if we come to consider of what material other gems are composed, we find that the ruby, sapphire, and other gem varieties of corundum, consist of alumina, which is certainly not less common than carbon, as it forms the basis of all clay and other like deposits, while the majority of the remaining gems consist largely of silica of which the greater portion of rocks principally consist.

Simple forms of the Cubical system.

The diamond crystallizes in the cubical system, that is, it has three imaginary axes all at right angles to each other, and all of the same length. The *octahedron* is the primary form, and this may be considered as composed of two four-sided pyramids placed base to base, with the axes joining each of the solid angles (a solid angle is the meeting of more than two faces.)

Placing six square planes equal to the length of one of the axes upon the solid angles of the octahedron, a six-sided figure is obtained, called a *cube* or *hexahedron*, having six equal faces, the axes being of the same length, and joining the faces of the cube in their centre.

If twelve planes are placed upon the edges of the octahedron (an edge being a line joining two faces), and extending these faces until they meet, a twelve-sided figure is obtained, called a *rhombic dodecahedron*, having twelve faces, and each face a rhombus.   It will be easily understood that the axes in this figure are all of the same length, and that it therefore belongs to the cubical system.   This figure is a common one for garnets, all of which crystallize in this system. These, the most simple forms of the cubical system, are easily distinguished ; models can be easily cut from some soft substance, a potato for instance.   The appearance is also shown in the diagram.

It is possible to have a portion of each of these three forms developed in the same crystal, but the axes will not vary in length.   A crystal having these faces developed might at first sight be considered a complex form, but it is not so, little consideration being necessary to identify the faces.

Instead of entirely removing the form of the octahedron, as in the cube and the rhombic dodecahedron, crystals are often found with other faces formed upon the octahedron. One form having three faces thus developed is called a *triakis octahedron* ; it has twenty-four small faces, each being an isosceles triangle, and they form obtuse three-sided pyramids over each face of the octahedron.

A figure having six small faces developed on each face of the octahedron is called a *hexakis octahedron* for that reason ; it has forty-eight faces, and is not an uncommon form of the diamond.

By placing obtuse four-sided pyramids upon each of the six faces of the cube a figure is obtained called a *tetrakis hexahedron*, or four-faced cube ; it is bounded by twenty-four equal isosceles triangles.

These are the principal *holohedral* forms of the cubical system (meaning those which possess the highest degree of symmetry of which the system admits), necessary to be known in the discrimination of gems, although perhaps the *icositetrahedron* should not be omitted, as it is common in garnet and leucite.   In general appearance this form somewhat resembles the triakis octahedron, but its faces are deltoid in shape, and each solid angle only joins four faces, while in the triakis octahedron eight meet together. This figure, which is also known as the *deltohedron*, has twenty-four faces.

Unfortunately for the simplicity of crystallography, *hemihedral* forms introduce themselves (that is, those which may be derived from a holohedral form by supposing half of the faces of the latter omitted according to a certain law). These figures are formed by enlarging each alternate face, or group of faces, to the removal of the intermediate ones; the hemihedral form, derived from the octahedron by suppressing each alternate face and extending the remainder, is called a *tetrahedron*, it has four triangular faces.

The *hexakis tetrahedron* is one hemihedral form of the hexakis octahedron and is formed by the same mode of replacement.

These hemihedral forms are not of very frequent occurrence in crystallized gems, although found in the diamond occasionally, so that it is well not to ignore them entirely.

More complex forms still are those known as twins, or twin-crystals, but not being of very frequent occurrence in gems, it will be unnecessary to describe their formation and appearance.

The edges of many of the crystals of diamonds are curved, giving the gem a spherical appearance more or less marked.

I have described thus fully the principal forms belonging to the cubical system, because the diamond usually takes one or the other of them, and the description will be sufficient for all those gems crystallizing in this system.

Large Diamonds.

There are in the Museum collection glass models of fourteen large historical diamonds, of which a short history is given here, as much interest is taken in them by the general public.

The "Regent" or "Pitt" diamond is a beautiful gem. It is an Indian stone, and was found by a slave in the Parteal mines on the River Kistna, in the year 1701; he is supposed to have concealed it, and it is reported to have also come into the possession of an Englishman in an unfair manner. It was bought by Mr. Pitt, Governor of Fort St. George, for £20,400, from a diamond merchant. It weighed in the rough 410 carats. It was cut in London, the process lasting two years, and thus reduced to 136¾ carats. It was sold to the Regent, Duke of Orleans, for £135,000, and thus passed into the possession of France. It was stolen, with other treasures, from the Garde Meuble, in 1792, and recovered in a peculiar manner. Napoleon wore it in the pommel of his sword. It is cut as a "brilliant," is inclined to the square form, and has been valued at £480,000. The model is 1¼ inch long, 1⅛ inch wide, and ¾ inch thick.

The "Koh-i-noor" or "Koh-i-nûr" diamond is now one of the Crown Jewels of England. It was named "Koh-i-nûr" by Nadir Shah ("Koh-i-nûr" means Mountain of Light) on first obtaining possession of the gem in 1739. It had long been in the possession of the Mogul dynasty. The origin of the stone is lost in antiquity. After many vicissitudes the gem was presented to Her Majesty Queen Victoria in 1850, through the East India Company. It had been cut, and then weighed 186½ carats. It was exhibited at the Great Exhibition in London, 1851. Was recut as a "brilliant," its present form, in 1852; now weighs 106½ carats; cost about £8,000 to recut. This diamond is kept at Windsor Castle, a model of the gem being kept in the jewel room at the Tower of London. Valued before recutting at £140,000. Models of the gem, both before and after recutting, are shown. Approximate measure—length, 1¼ inch, width, 1¼ inch, depth, ¾ inch.

The "Great Mogul" is supposed to be one of the largest diamonds ever found. Our knowledge of it is obtained from the account given by Tavernier, who saw it in India in 1665, and recorded its appearance in his work published in Paris, 1676 and 1682. It weighed in the rough 787½ carats, but had been cut by a European named Borgis, who reduced it in the cutting to its then weight, 279⅜ carats. Found at the Gani mine, in Golconda, India. Its present location unknown, all traces of it having been lost. A model is shown as it was seen by Tavernier; it somewhat resembles half an egg, nearly flat and quite smooth on the top, and a large number of facets covering the round portion. It is 1½ inch over the top, and 1⅛ inch deep.

The "Florentine" or "Austrian Yellow" diamond is a triangular stone, faceted on both sides, and is of a citron tint. It belonged to the Grand Duke of Tuscany during Tavernier's time, and was supposed to be then the largest diamond in Europe, but its yellowish colour detracts from its value. It weighs 139½ carats. It has been in the possession of Austria since the time of Maria Theresa. It is, judged by its mode of cutting, an Indian stone, and must have been brought from the East at an early date. It has been stated to have belonged to Charles the Bold, who lost it at the battle of Morat. Valued at various figures from £40,000 to £155,000. It is nearly 1 inch in thickness.

The "Nussak" diamond is so named from the town of Nussak, situated on the Upper Godavery, 95 miles by rail north-west of Bombay. Cave temples were situated here, and this gem is supposed to have been taken from the shrines by the Peishwas. When Bajerow the Peishwa surrendered to the British in 1818, this diamond was handed over to the Marquis of Hastings. It was triangular in shape, and weighed 89¾ carats. Sold by auction in London in 1820 for £7,200, an exceedingly low figure. It has been recut, its weight now being 78⅝ carats. It belongs to the Marquis of Westminster.

The "Hope Blue" diamond is of a beautiful colour, and weighs 44½ carats. It is cut as a "brilliant" of the square form. Tavernier brought a blue diamond with him from the East, which weighed 112¼ carats. This is supposed to be the original of the "French Blue," weighing 67¼ carats, and estimated to be valued at £120,000, by inventory of French Crown jewels drawn up in 1791. This was stolen with other treasures from the Garde Meuble in 1792, and from that time lost. The "Hope Blue" is supposed by Mr. Streeter to be a portion of this "French Blue" diamond. Purchased by Mr. Hope for £18,000, valued at £30,000. Now the property of the family of the Duke of Newcastle. It is 1 inch in length, ⅞ inch in width, and over ½ inch in thickness. It is understood that this gem is now for sale. An American lately offered 100,000 dollars for it, but the offer was refused.

The "Sancy" or "Great Sancy" diamond is an almond-shaped gem, faceted on both sides, indicating Indian workmanship. Belonged to M. de Sanci. Worn by Henry III of France. Afterwards passed into possession of Elizabeth Queen of England. Sold by James to Louis XIV for £25,000. Appears in the inventory of the French Crown jewels, 1791, valued at £40,000. Afterwards owned by Prince Paul Demidoff, who sold it, a wealthy merchant of Bombay, Sir Jamsetjee Jeejeebhoy, becoming the owner. Afterwards purchased by the Maharaja of Puttiala. It weighed 53¼ carats.

The "Eugénie" diamond is an oval stone, cut as a "brilliant," and was set as the centre of a hair-pin belonging to the Empress Catherine II of Russia. It was given by her to one of her favourites, named Potemkin, a niece of

B

whom sold it to the Emperor Napoleon III, who gave it to his wife, who gave it its present name. It was worn in a necklace, which after the Franco-German war, was sold to the Gaikwar of Baroda for £15,000. Its present owner is unknown. It weighs 51 carats.

The ' Orloff" diamond is much the shape of a portion of a small egg, faceted all over the round portion, with five irregular flat surfaces on the top. It is characteristic of Indian-cut diamonds, and inclined to the shape of the " Great Mogul." It was originally the eye of an idol in India, and was stolen by a French soldier who had deserted the Indian Service. He sold the gem to an English sea-captain for £2,000, who brought it to London and sold it for £12,000. Prince Orloff bought the gem at Amsterdam for £90,000 cash and an annuity of £4,000. He presented it to Catherine II of Russia. It has been valued at about £390,000. It belongs to Russia, and weighs 194¼ carats. Its weight uncut is not known.

The "Star of the South" diamond was found by a negress at work at the mines of the Minas-Geraes, Brazil, July, 1853. Her lucky find secured her her freedom and a small pension as well. The stone weighed in the rough 254½ carats, and was sold as found for £35,000. It was cut at Mr. Coster's establishment at Amsterdam, and reduced to 125 carats. It is cut as a "brilliant," and is 1⅜ inch long, 1⅛ inch wide, and ⅞ inch thick. It is more square than the Koh-i-noor. Exhibited at the London Exhibition, 1862, and at Paris in 1867 ; £110,000 was offered for it and refused, but it was eventually sold to the Gaikwar of Baroda, India, for 8 lakhs of rupees (£80,000).

The "Pigott" diamond was so named after Mr. Pigott, Governor of Madras, afterwards Lord Pigott. Sold by lottery in 1801, and won by a young man, who sold it for a low price. Bought by Ali Pasha afterwards for £30,000, who, when mortally wounded, ordered the diamond to be crushed to powder in his presence. This was done, and this beautiful gem thus destroyed, the model alone remaining. It was an Indian stone, but exact locality unknown. Weight given differently by various writers—Mawe at 49 carats, Emanuel at 82¼. The size of the model would indicate the latter figure. It is 1¼ inch long, 1 inch wide, and over ½ inch in thickness.

The "Shah " diamond, is a peculiar shaped gem, long, narrow, and having few facets ; it is one of the few diamonds that have been engraved. It is supposed to have formed part of the Persian regalia from the remotest times. Its weight is 86 carats, and its weight before cutting was 95 carats. It now belongs to Russia. It is 1½ inch in length, ¾ inch in width, and ⅛ inch in thickness.

The " Polar Star" diamond is cut as a "brilliant," of the square form. It weighs 40¼ carats, it belongs to Russia. It was purchased in England for the Imperial regalia, it has a very fine lustre.

The "Pasha of Egypt" diamond is cut as a "brilliant," round in shape. It was purchased by Ibrahim Pasha for £28,000. It weighs 40 carats. Present locality not known for certain.

Of late years several large diamonds have been found in the South African mines. One very large irregular crystal inclining to the octahedral form was found in the De Beer's mine. It weighed 428½ carats in the rough. It was cut and exhibited in the Paris Exhibition of 1889. It weighed, after cutting, 228½ carats, thus losing 200 carats in the process.

What is perhaps the largest and most valuable diamond in the world was, however, found on July 30th, 1893, in the Jagersfontein mine. Its weight in the rough is 969½ carats, the colour is blue-white, and it is of fine quality.

Its value cannot be estimated. This diamond was obtained at a cost of 8 dollars per carat, for it was obtained under contract with a lot of other stones. Had it not been discovered until six hours later those who secured it would not have received it, for the contract would have expired.

The "Porter-Rhodes" diamond was found Feb. 12th, 1880, in the Kimberley mine. It weighed in the rough 150 carats, and its estimated value is £200,000. It is of a very fine lustre.

The "Stewart" diamond was one of the earliest large diamonds found in the South African fields, its weight in the rough was 288¾ carats. It is of a light yellow tinge. It was found in the year 1872.

The "Jagersfontein," a diamond weighing, in the rough, 209¼ carats was obtained in this locality; it was stolen, but recovered by the owner.

The "Du Toit I" and "Du Toit II," the first a gem weighing 244 carats when cut, the other weighed in the rough 124 carats. These were obtained at Du Toit's Pan.

The "Star of South Africa," better known as the "Dudley," weighed in the rough 83½ carats, by cutting it was reduced to 46½ carats. It is the property of the Countess of Dudley. It is the diamond obtained by Van Niekirk from a native in the early days of the diamond fields.

Besides this list, there are a great many other large diamonds of historical interest that have been obtained from the various diamond fields of the world, many of these gems are connected with deeds of crime of the worst character.

CORUNDUM,

and its gem varieties, Ruby, Sapphire, Amethyst, Emerald, Topaz, Aquamarine, and Asteria.

To distinguish these from other minerals bearing the same names they are known as Oriental, thus: "Oriental topaz," "Oriental amethyst," "Oriental emerald," "Oriental aquamarine," and "Oriental ruby."

Originally the words Oriental and Occidental were applied literally, but now they are used to simply establish the superior quality of the gem or otherwise, so that Oriental ruby means the true ruby.

Crystalline system = Hexagonal.

Hardness = 9.

Specific gravity = 3·9—4·16.

Lustre = Vitreous, sometimes pearly on the basal planes.

Cleavage = Basal; that is at right angles to the principal axis of the prism, sometimes perfect.

Composition = Pure Alumina ($Al_2 O_3$) Aluminium 53·4, Oxygen 46·6 per cent.

Inferior corundum (not considering emery) contains in some instances as much as 15 per cent. of impurities, these being iron, lime, magnesia, and silica.

From a mineralogical point of view the different colours of the varieties of corundum are of no account, as it is the physical properties and chemical composition that determine the species, and chemistry has not yet enabled us to arrive at a satisfactory conclusion as to the cause of the differences of colour in the several varieties of this mineral. That the colour is derived from the presence of minute quantities of metallic oxides appear certain, but this does not account for the blue colour of the sapphire, or the red of the ruby; yet it is these very colours that determine the value of these gems and assists to place them in the category of precious stones.

The material of which they are principally composed is one of the most plentiful of the constituents of the earth's crust. As silicate of alumina in clay it exists in its most plentiful and useful form, while in the ruby we find it as the most rare and costly of all the treasures of the earth.

Corundum does not appear to have been considered of much scientific interest until the latter part of the eighteenth century, although it had been used for dressing stones four thousand years before. It was, until late years, invariably obtained from surface washings; but a remarkable deposit having been found in Macon County, North Carolina, this mineral has, since the year 1872, been systematically mined there. It occurs in veins running through serpentine.

The peculiarity of the corundums from this locality is that they exhibit in some specimens several hues in the same stone. Some very large crystals have been found in these veins; one weighing 312 lb. is in the cabinet of Amherst College, U.S.A.

Nine different varieties of corundum have been taken from these mines since they were first opened, and the discovery is of the greatest importance, as both rubies and sapphires were there found *in situ* in good quantities, and, according to Mr. Streeter, this is the only known instance of their being thus found.

Geological Formation.—Corundum is found usually in beds of rivers, as water-worn crystals, and is often associated with other precious stones, several of its varieties being found in the diamondiferous drifts of this Colony. In India it is principally found in the old crystalline or metamorphic rocks, and it is from the southern portion of that country that the greatest quantity of corundum is obtained. (Our modern name corundum is derived from the Hindoo word *Kurand*). Mr. Mallet has given an account of a remarkable mine in India, where he states that above a mass of porphyritic gneiss and hornblende rock, there lies a bed of corundum several yards thick, and of a reddish and purple grey colour; upon this rests a bed of white and green jade, with purple corundum and other minerals. At St. Gothard (Switzerland) it occurs of a red and blue colour in dolomite, and near Mozzo, in Piedmont, in white compact feldspar. In America it occurs in Maine, at Greenwood, crystallized in mica-schist, with beryl and zircon, and at other localities in granular limestone; so that its distribution throughout the older rocks is well marked, and it is not restricted to any one formation. It is sometimes found in basalt, and is stated to so occur in this Colony. It is very probable that good specimens of coloured corundums will eventually be obtained from Central Queensland. I have seen some from that locality changing in portions to blue, and of good size.

Coloured corundums are invariably dichroic, and are thus easy of determination, as will be shown under the variety ruby.

Friction excites electricity, and in polished specimens the electrical attraction continues for a long time.

Ordinary solvents have no action upon this mineral.

Corundums crystallize principally in double hexagonal pyramids, that is, having two pyramids, each with six faces, placed base to base. These pyramids are more elongated than those of quartz crystals. A portion of the prism may separate the pyramids.

We will consider the word corundum to be appropriated by the common varieties, having a grey, greenish or reddish colour, and which are dull, and pass on to the gem varieties. The brown variety is known as *Adamantine Spar*.

Ruby, Oriental Ruby, or Red Sapphire.

This, when of perfect colour and of fair size, is more valuable than any other precious stone. If a diamond of 5 carats be worth £350, a faultless ruby of the same weight would be worth quite £3,000. The value of these gems above that weight increases in proportion, and, according to Mr. Streeter, a perfect ruby of 10 carats is almost invaluable. He says that a perfect stone of 5 carats will fetch ten times as much as a diamond of the same weight. The number of fine large rubies of undoubted genuineness is small, though there are on record several gems of immense size reputed to be rubies. Nearly all the great historic rubies now extant have been pronounced spinels, and Mr. Emanuel states that the two large stones shown amongst the jewels of her Majesty at the London Exhibition of 1862 as rubies, are simply spinels.

The difference between these two gems is easy of determination, and there should be no uncertainty about the matter, although the colour of spinel often approaches that of the ruby, yet the property of dichroism that the ruby has is wanting in the spinel, and at once distinguishes it from that mineral. Those gems crystallizing in the cubical system, when viewed through the dichroiscope, do not exhibit the property of dichroism, and the spinel crystallizes in this system; while the ruby, which crystallizes in the hexagonal system, when tested with this instrument invariably gives the two squares of different hues, or shows dichroism. This test also distinguishes the ruby from the garnet, as the latter is also cubical. Besides this test of dichroism, spinel may be distinguished from the ruby by its deficient hardness (corundum scratching it), and by the lower specific gravity of spinel. The specific gravity of the garnet does not differ much in some instances from that of the ruby, but it is much inferior in hardness, and it is fusible in the blowpipe flame, ruby being infusible.

All the fine rubies are supposed to have come from Burmah; at any rate, two authenticated gems from that country reached Europe in 1875. When recut they weighed 32⅛ and 39⅝ carats respectively, the larger one being sold for £20,000. The necessities of the Burmese Government were the cause of their transference to Europe.

The ruby mines of Burmah being a Royal monopoly, all persons finding rubies over a certain weight were bound, under penalty of death, to deliver them to the Government. It is very probable that many stones of large size have been reduced to smaller portions to prevent their being handed over, thus causing loss to the country and the Government.

There appears to be little doubt that the Royal Treasury of Burmah contains some large and beautiful rubies; these most probably will find their way eventually to the European market.

Rubies are also obtained from Ceylon, the Chinese provinces bordering upon the Burmese Empire, from Tartary, Siam, and in smaller quantities from several other localities.

The rubies that are now being obtained in large quantities in Siam, are considered to be of an inferior colour to those from Burmah, but the author was assured by a gentleman connected with the Siam mines, that this difficulty of colour is got over by transferring them first to Burmah, and then forwarding them to Europe as stones from the latter country.

It is a well known fact that when the diamond was first obtained from Brazil in large quantities, a similar prejudice arose against these gems, but the difficulty was got over in that instance by first shipping them to India, and then to Europe as Indian diamonds.

The rubies are obtained in Siam by the natives washing the alluvial deposit that contains them. This washing is carried on in a most primitive way with the dish. Large numbers of natives are thus employed.

I am informed that at the locality where the rubies are obtained, the formation is as follows :—Surface soil, 1 foot ; under this a sandy clay, from which the gems are obtained ; then pure clay upon metamorphic rock, overlying basalt. The majority of the stones are small, a large one being rarely obtained. The rubies are plentiful. They are principally used by watchmakers. The neighbouring hills are principally an igneous rock, and there appears little doubt but that this rock is the matrix of these gems.

The hardness of the gem varieties of corundum is such that they are only scratched by the diamond ; and partly for that reason an engraved ruby was looked upon with admiration. At the London Exhibition of 1851 there were two engraved rubies belonging to the Hope collection, one representing the head of Jupiter-Serapis, the other a full length figure of Minerva-Poliada. A good many other engraved rubies are recorded, but some of these probably are not genuine.

The ruby is cut by means of diamond powder on an iron wheel, and polished on a copper one with tripoli and water. In the East, corundum wheels are used for the cutting. The best stones are usually cut with facets, but imperfect ones are cut *en cabochon* (*see* plate, "Forms of cutting precious stones "), that is, with a convex surface without facets. The slippers of Chinese and Indian ladies are often ornamented with rubies, cut *en cabochon*, and a large quantity were at one time used to ornament the armour, scabbards, and harness, of nobles and others in India and China. In fact, the ruby has always been highly esteemed in Oriental countries, being regarded as endowed with more than ordinary properties, even being laid beneath the foundation of buildings, to secure good fortune to the structure.

In New South Wales a few rubies only have been obtained at the localities given below, although no doubt a large number have been overlooked by miners under the impression that they were garnets. Those found have been small, and always in "drifts."

Considering the importance and value of the ruby, it would be judicious in all cases to ascertain the identity of red stones. The expression "better be sure than sorry " is very apt.

The importance of correct nomenclature in gems is well illustrated in the case of the supposed rubies from South Australia. The finding of these *garnets* caused some excitement at the time, although no mineralogist would consider them anything but garnets. They are dark, deficient in hardness, *fusible*, and are not dichroic. There is an educational set of these garnets in the Museum collection.

The following are the localities in this Colony where rubies have been found :—

> County Phillip.—Cudgegong River, Great Mullen Creek, Lawson's Creek, Rats' Castle Creek, between Eumbi and Bimbijong.
> „   Wellington.—Bald Hills, Mudgee.
> „   Wynyard.—Tumberumba.

A variety of the ruby, called Barklyite, has been found at Two-mile Flat, Cudgegong, New South Wales, and by Mr. Porter, at New England.

The specimens of this purple or magenta coloured opaque corundum in the Museum collection, all came from the Ovens, in Victoria. The hardness is a little less than 9, sapphire just scratching it. There is no external signs of crystalline form in these specimens. One rolled pebble weighs 3·915 grams., another specimen weighs 8·286 grams., while a third weighs 1·7014 grams. These have an average specific gravity of 3·9095.

The ruby has been made artificially by M. Fremy, of Paris, who succeeded in manufacturing these gems of sufficient size to be used by watchmakers for jewelling watches. I do not know the value of these artificial rubies, or whether they can be made a financial success.

Sapphire or Oriental Sapphire.

Of all the gem varieties of corundum the blue sapphire is perhaps the most plentiful ; yet, although found in good quantity in many parts of the world, few large stones of good colour are obtainable. The value of the sapphire does not increase in proportion to its size, as is the case with the ruby, although large sums have been paid for specimens at different times. The celebrated gem in the mineral collection of the Jardin des Plantes, in Paris, weighs 133⅛ carats, and is without a fault. It was originally found in Bengal (India) by a poor man, came into the possession of a German prince, and was by him sold to a French jewel merchant for £6,800.

Two fine stones were exhibited in the London Exhibition of 1862. The larger weighed about 252 carats ; the smaller, and more beautiful one, was brought from India, and after being recut weighed 165 carats. It is supposed to be the most valuable sapphire in Europe, its estimated value being £7,000 to £8,000.

Among the historic sapphires (of which there are a great many) may be mentioned the gem, cut in the form of a rose, once owned by Edward the Confessor, and which now ornaments the Royal Crown of England. Another fine sapphire in the same crown was purchased by George IV. It was originally a sapphire ring taken from the finger of Queen Elizabeth just after she expired, and was sent to James VI. of Scotland as a token of his accession to the English throne.

Many of the treasuries of Europe possess very valuable sapphires, especially that of Russia.

The value of a perfect sapphire of one carat is worth as much as a perfect brilliant (diamond) of the same weight. To be perfect it must be of a deep, rich blue colour by night as well as by day, because it is a defect that the sapphire often has, of becoming an indifferent colour by artificial light. The value of good stones is such, that in a country like New South Wales, where sapphires are plentifully distributed, some attention should be given to the collection of good, clear, bright blue stones.

Engraved sapphires were at one time considered of the greatest value, a gem in the collection of the Duke of Brunswick being engraved with the arms of England, formerly belonged to Mary Queen of Scots. A sapphire beautifully engraved with the crest and arms of Cardinal Wolsey has been recently found in an old collection of jewels In the British Museum there is a statue of Buddha cut from a single sapphire.

During the Renaissance period engraved gems became fashionable, and many engravings of white sapphire and white topaz were for a long time considered as engraved diamonds. Occasionally sapphires may be made colourless by heating them, and these white stones do acquire great brilliancy, sufficient to deceive a casual observer. The differences between these gems have been already stated in the article on the diamond.

The blue stones that might be taken for sapphire are kyanite, iolite, blue tourmaline, and blue beryl.

Kyanite, which is a silicate of alumina, is much softer and of less specific gravity, besides belonging to a different crystalline system.

Iolite, which is also one of the silicates, may easily be distinguished from the sapphire by its less specific gravity, its deficient hardness, and its *fusibility.*

Blue tourmaline, which is cut as a gem and known as Brazilian sapphire, is distinguished by its deficient hardness and its less specific gravity.

Blue beryl is hardly to be mistaken for the sapphire, but if the resemblance is great it may be distinguished by the same tests.

Glass imitations are more deceptive, though greatly deficient in hardness, and wanting in dichroism. This property of the sapphire is very marked, the best stones giving squares—one deep ultramarine, the other greenish straw-yellow.

The ancients of the time of Pliny included under the term *sapphirus* the blue stone known as lapis-lazuli, and from which ultramarine was originally made, while the probability is that the name of our sapphire was *hyacinthus*, as it is stated by Solinus, a connoisseur of gems, who wrote two centuries after Pliny, that this stone, of a shining blue colour, was not adapted for engraving, as it defied all grinding, and was only cut into shape by the diamond. This could only apply to the blue corundum, or sapphire.

The sapphire was considered to be endowed with supernatural powers to a greater extent even than the ruby; it was sacred to the good Apollo, being worn by those inquiring of the oracle at his shrine. Altogether, the superstitious reverence given to this stone was greater than in that of any other gem.

The best sapphires have been found in India and Ceylon, but this gem is found in all localities where the ruby and other gem varieties of corundum are obtained; some fine ones have been found in Burmah and Siam.

In the year 1878, a blue sapphire was found in Ceylon, weighing 2½lb., about 4,560 carats, but it was of a light-blue colour, and contained many flaws.

The composition, hardness, crystalline form, and specific gravity are the same as in the ruby, the only difference being the colour. The most approved shade of the sapphire is "royal blue."

In the colony of New South Wales sapphires are almost invariably found in auriferous drifts; they are usually much waterworn, and very dark-coloured specimens unfortunately predominate, although all tints and shades of blue are occasionally found, and these often in the same stone. The majority are small and of little value, but there is no reason to doubt that fine valuable stones do exist, and only require searching for. Mr. Streeter states that he has lately received a sapphire from Australia weighing just under 100 carats, and several over 50 carats. Unfortunately the quality of these stones was not of the best; they were too dark, and do not show the true blue of the sapphire. In certain parts of the colony they are said to exist in basalt. It is a fact that they do so, near Emmaville, so that it may be considered that in this locality the matrix of the sapphire is basalt. This is no new home of this gem.

A very large number of localities have been recorded for the sapphire in this colony. It would be tedious, perhaps, to enumerate them all, but it may be taken as a general rule that where auriferous drifts occur, sapphires may be found. It has been found in many places in the following counties:— Camden, Clarke, Darling, Georgiana, Gough, Wellington, Wynyard, Hardinge, Inglis, Murchison, Northumberland, Parry, Phillip, Roxburgh, Sandon and Wallace.

Oriental Amethyst, or Purple Sapphire.

This is the true amethyst, and is distinguished by its amethystine or purple colour. The name amethyst is now generally given to the purple variety of quartz, and it is as well to bear this in mind, because the quartz amethyst is comparatively a common mineral, and not of much value, while the purple corundum (the true amethyst) is rare, and far more valuable. The difference in hardness and specific gravity will readily determine these minerals, besides the quartz variety has less brilliancy.

There are fine specimens of the oriental amethyst at Dresden (Germany), and in the Vatican are engraved intaglios of this gem, of a very early date.

Oriental amethyst has not yet been recorded from New South Wales.

Oriental Emerald, or Green Sapphire.

This is the green variety of corundum, and must not be mistaken for the emerald, which is a totally different mineral. When of good colour, it is greatly superior in brilliancy and lustre to the ordinary emerald, and on account of its hardness and great rarity, is far more valuable. The oriental emerald is stated to be fairly plentiful in Northern Gippsland, Victoria. At the Melbourne Exhibition of 1888, Professor Liversidge exhibited two cut specimens of this gem; these were found at Bingera, in this colony. Greenish sapphires are not uncommon in the New England district of this Colony.

Oriental Aquamarine.

When the green variety of corundum is very pale coloured, it is called oriental aquamarine. It is distinguished from the ordinary aquamarine (which is a variety of the beryl), by its superior hardness and specific gravity, and by being far more brilliant. When the tint is inclining to olive, this stone is known by the name of oriental peridot.

Oriental Topaz, or Yellow Sapphire.

This variety of corundum is more plentiful than the green and purple varieties; it is of a yellow tint, generally inclining to a light straw-colour; it is a very brilliant stone, but of little value commercially. It, and the yellow diamond, might be mistaken for each other; but the difference in hardness and in crystalline form distinguishes them. Oriental topaz also usually shows dichroism, which property is wanting in the diamond. Its difference from yellow zircon may be determined by the inferior hardness of the latter, by the difference in crystalline form, and other tests.

Asteria, or Star Stone.

This name was given by the ancients to certain species of precious stones, principally corundums, which, having a peculiar structure, displayed rays of light in the form of a six-pointed star.

Romantic people placed a high value upon these star-stones, considering them a powerful love charm, and tradition tells us that one in a signet ring was worn by Helen of Homeric fame, so that it is not improbable that this asteria was connected (although no doubt unintentionally) with the calamities of the Trojan war.

If the star corundum is blue it is a star-sapphire, if red a star-ruby, and so on.

Star-sapphires are very plentiful in the New England district of this Colony, although usually of too dark colour for cutting purposes.

These gems are best cut *en cabochon*, care being taken to get the centre of the star in the middle of the convex surface.

It is only of late years that these star stones have come into fashion in Europe. Not many years ago they could have been purchased in Ceylon for small sums, but star rubies at the present time, if of good quality, fetch high prices; being rare they are highly prized.

In the Hope collection there were six asterias of a very high character. Of course, the value of these gems is determined by their size and quality. Star sapphires range from £2 to £100; star rubies are still more valuable.

Besides the ornamental uses to which these gems are put, there is that of the more important one in connection with manufacture. That this item of consumption is not an insignificant one, may be judged from the fact that in the United States of America, where the watch industry is of great magnitude, the consumption of gems alone for the jewelled works of the watches manufactured in that country, cannot be less than 12,000,000 annually, of which nearly half are rubies and sapphires, the remainder being principally garnets. The consumption, too, of "bort," used in the drilling and working of these gems, reaches many thousand carats per annum.

It is, of course, not necessary that these gems be of large size, but it is important that they be free from flaws, of good colour, transparent, and of the correct hardness.

In the New England district of this Colony, sapphires are plentiful, and although, unfortunately, many are very dark and opaque, yet very many bright, clear gems may be gathered of good colour, transparent, and correct hardness. Many of these transparent corundums, too, are of a green colour (inferior Oriental emeralds), and these should not be discarded. As the greater part of the gems used in America for watch-making purposes are imported, and the whole of those used in England, the collection of these gems is a matter worthy of some consideration.

Simple Forms of the Hexagonal System.

As all the varieties of corundum crystallize in the hexagonal system, it will be as well to consider the most simple of the forms belonging to it.

In this system (unlike all the others) there are four axes; one, the principal, has no fixed length, the remaining three lie at right angles to the principal axis in one plane, and they are inclined to each other at an angle at 60 degrees. This plane, by joining the three axes, forms a hexagon, these axes being all the same length.

The primary form of this system is the *hexagonal pyramid* (two six-sided pyramids placed base to base), all the other forms being derived from it. In this form the principal axis joins the two six-sided solid angles (refer to the cubical system in the article diamond for the meaning of terms), the lateral axes joining the lateral solid angles if belonging to the first order, and the centre of the lateral edges if belonging to the second order. (These orders are only of importance in combinations.) It has twelve faces, these being isosceles triangles, and they are acute or obtuse as the principal axis is long or short. This is a common form of the corundum.

HEXAGONAL SYSTEM.
Simple forms.

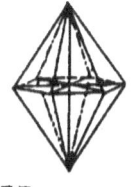

Hexagonal
Pyramid.

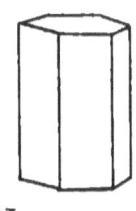

Hexagonal
Prism.

Dihexagonal
Pyramid.

Dihexagonal
Prism.

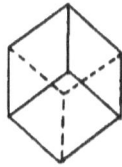

Rhombohedron.

Hexagonal
Scalenohedron.

(5 a 201-35-6)

If six planes are placed parallel to the principal axis of the hexagonal pyramid, allowing the lateral axes to join the edges (if the first order), or the centre of the planes (if the second order), and closing the figure with two hexagons, we get a form called a *hexagonal prism*. This form is bounded by six rectangles and two regular hexagons, or the ends of the prism may be closed by other forms in combination ; a hexagonal pyramid, for instance, as is often seen in quartz crystals.

The *dihexagonal pyramid* has double the number of faces, or twenty-four equal isosceles triangles, if the form is a compound of the first and second orders of pyramids.

The *dihexagonal prism* has twelve rectangular faces and the basal planes are dodecahedral. This form has been identified with corundum.

These are the principal holohedral forms belonging to the hexagonal system.

There are two hemihedral forms belonging to this system often found in minerals ; the most important is the *rhombohedron.* This is formed by extending each alternate face of the hexagonal pyramid to the exclusion of the others. The figure may be either obtuse or acute, this depending on the original form of the pyramid. It is bounded by six rhombic planes, and the principal axis joins the two equal three-sided solid angles.

The *hexagonal scalenohedron* is the hemihedral form of the dihexagonal pyramid. It is formed by the suppression of alternate *pairs* of faces, and not alternate faces as in the rhombohedron ; it is bounded by twelve scalene triangles.

This system is a very beautiful and complicated one, although the numerous combinations do not interest us in the study of precious stones.

It should not be difficult for anyone to distinguish gems crystallizing in the above forms of the hexagonal system, although it is hardly to be expected that natural gems will give the perfect symmetrical forms as illustrated above. When found in alluvial deposits the edges of the crystals are usually more or less worn or abraded.

BERYL,

and its Varieties, Aquamarine and Emerald.

Crystalline system—Hexagonal.
Hardness—7·5—8.
Specific gravity—2·63—2·75.
Lustre—Vitreous to resinous.
Cleavage—Parallel to the basal plane, rather indistinct.
Composition—Silicate of Alumina and Beryllia (Glucina).
3 BeO SiO_2 + Al_2O_3, $3SiO_2$.
Silica—66·8, Alumina—19·1, Beryllia—14·1 per cent.
The colours of this mineral are—emerald green, pale green, light blue, yellow, and white.

It is one of the few minerals which occurs only in crystals, and that has no essential variations in chemical composition.

Crystals have been found of enormous dimensions. One shown at the London Exhibition of 1851 weighed 80 lb., but this must be considered quite small in comparison with some crystals found at Grafton, New

Hampshire, North America. One from this locality weighed 2,900 pounds avoirdupois. It was 4 ft. 3 in. long, 32 inches in one direction, and 22 inches in another, transverse to the last across the crystal. Another specimen weighed 1,070 pounds. A still larger crystal from the same locality was estimated to weigh 2½ tons. It seems almost incredible that the arrangement of the molecules of this compound substance in regular geometrical forms, should be carried out to such an extent in any one specimen. These large crystals are generally muddy in appearance, and portions are almost opaque, although large specimens are sometimes found perfectly transparent. One, an aquamarine weighing 225 troy ounces and without a flaw, belonged to the late Emperor of Brazil, and some of the Russian aquamarines and transparent or precious beryls are of large size.

The ancients obtained the beryl first from India, then from Arabia, and later from Siberia. It was used for engraving by the Greeks more than two thousand years ago, and by the Romans at a later period. The beryl has been stated to have been the only gem cut with facets by the Roman lapidaries. There is a fine specimen of an engraved beryl in the British Museum consisting of a Cupid on a dolphin. One of the finest beryls known, a gem from India, belonged to the Hope collection; it weighed 6½ ounces. A magnificent blue beryl surmounts the globe in the Royal Crown of Great Britain.

The commercial value of the beryl is small. It is used in England principally for cheap jewellery or to ornament metal work. The yellow variety is sometimes called chrysolite, although quite a different mineral from the true chrysolite; the hardness, specific gravity, and crystalline form of these two minerals being quite distinct.

Aquamarine.

This name was given to precious stones supposed to resemble in colour the water of the sea, as the name denotes. The beryl having this colour is less valuable than the emerald, although it has the property of retaining its brilliancy by artificial light. There is little reason why this gem should be considered a distinct variety of the beryl, as the line of demarcation is less marked than in that of the emerald, but as several aquamarines of considerable value have been recorded it is perhaps as well to retain the distinction. This variety of the beryl occurs in many localities, but the greater portion used in jewellery comes from India, the Ural Mountains, and Brazil. A specimen found in Russia in 1827 was stated to have been valued at about £20,000.

The historical aquamarine that once adorned the tiara of Pope Julius II, having passed into the possession of the French, was placed in the Museum of Natural History in Paris, where it remained for more than three centuries. It was then returned to the Vatican by Napoleon I, and presented to Pope Pius VII. It is of a beautiful sea-green colour, and is about 2 inches in length by about the same in thickness. An intaglio cut from an aquamarine was presented to the Abbey of Saint Denys by Charlemagne, where it ornamented a gold reliquary; it is now in the National Library of Paris. It is engraved with the portrait of Julia, the daughter of the Emperor Titus.

An aquamarine weighing 3½ ounces ornamented the hilt of Murat's sword, now in the South Kensington Museum.

Emerald.

This is the bright, transparent, dark green variety of the beryl. It has been highly prized from the earliest times as a gem-stone, on account of its great brilliancy and beauty. It has always maintained its position as one of the most desirable stones for ornamental purposes, and there is no doubt about its use in the most remote ages. Necklaces of emeralds have been found at Herculaneum and at other places.

The Orientals have always had a great veneration for these gems; they believed that they had the power to impart courage to the wearer, and to protect one from the plague. The ancients supposed them to be good for the eyes, and to be a remedy for various diseases.

The natives of Peru venerated the emerald as the abode of their favourite divinity. The chief goddess of Peru was supposed to be an emerald, and the principal offerings made to it consisted of this gem. During the invasion of Mexico the Spaniards carried off immense quantities of emeralds, many of which found their way into the Royal Treasury of Spain. After the conquest of the New World these gems became very plentiful, and were in great demand. The Dresden Museum contains a large uncut emerald, while the collection at Munich has several of large size; these were from Peru. The treasury of Russia contains many fine emeralds, and the Crown jewels of many countries are more or less ornamented with these gems.

In the London Exhibition of 1851 there was shown a very fine emerald of a beautiful colour; it was 2 inches in length, and across the three diameters measured $2\frac{1}{4}$, $2\frac{1}{3}$, and $1\frac{7}{8}$ inches respectively. Its weight was 8 oz. 18 dwt. This emerald was obtained at Muzo, near Santa Fé de Bogota, in South America. It was taken to England by Dom Pedro, from whom it was purchased by the Duke of Devonshire.

A splendid girdle of an Indian chief was also shown at the same exhibition, made of slices from a large and beautiful emerald, advantage having been taken of the natural basal cleavage of this mineral. These slices were surrounded by diamonds, some of which were in their natural state. The slices of the emerald in this girdle were $\frac{1}{4}$ of an inch in thickness. This was the mode of mounting this gem previous to the year 1456, so that, without doubt, this girdle was manufactured previous to that date.

There is a magnificent specimen in the Townshend collection; it is perfect in colour, and measures $\frac{1}{2}$ an inch across. Many other historical emeralds might be mentioned, but the above are sufficient to illustrate the great value placed upon these gems by the people of many countries for centuries past.

Mr. Streeter states that the value of the emerald ranges from 5s. a carat for very light coloured stones, up to £50 to £60 a carat for very fine dark coloured gems without flaws. These last are very rare, because the emerald is so rarely found perfect, that "an emerald without a flaw" has become a common expression. The basal cleavage, too, is often detrimental to good stones, and the precaution is taken of keeping them from the light.for some time after removal from the mine.

It is generally supposed that the name "Emerald Isle," as given to Ireland, is because of its remarkably green verdure, but the name is also in some measure connected with the emerald itself. Pope Adrian IV, when he issued his famous Bull in 1156, granting the sovereignty over the island to the King of England, is stated to have sent to Henry II a ring set with an emerald, as the instrument of his investiture with the dominion of the island.

The substances most resembling the emerald are green spinel, green glass, green garnets, and green sapphires. The former is easily distinguished by its higher specific gravity, and by its crystallizing in the cubical system (the emerald crystallizing in the hexagonal system). The difference between the emerald and green glass is easy of determination, the inferior hardness of glass and its want of dichroism being sufficient for this purpose. The dichroism of the emerald is very strong; when viewed across the prism with the dichroiscope, the two squares are seen to be of different hues of green. The aquamarine is also dichroic. The higher specific gravity is sufficient to determine the green garnets, while the superior hardness will distinguish the green sapphires.

The Cingalese are stated to manufacture "genuine emeralds" for foreigners, from green glass bottles, and the "Brighton emeralds" have a similar origin. Some of the historical gigantic emeralds of the middle ages have been unable to stand the tests of modern mineralogists, and have been found to consist of green glass.

The colouring matter of the emerald has been the cause of much inquiry, but the general opinion is that it is from the presence of chromium. According to Lewy, the emeralds from Muzo become white at a red heat, and from his experiments he arrived at the conclusion that the colouring material was organic. These results have not been confirmed by later chemists, and chromic oxide is now considered as the colouring agent.

The emerald is usually "step" or "trap" cut, the table not being too large. This technical term is used for that style of cutting gems, where the facets run around the stone, which is generally longer than broad, the flat portion at the top being called the table.

Emeralds, and the other varieties of the beryl, are found in many different geological formations. In Siberia the emerald is found in mica schist. In the Urals it occurs in large crystals, together with chrysoberyl and phenacite in a micaceous schist forming a group of rocks situated to the north-east of Ekaterinburg. Some of the large beryl crystals found in North America are embedded in quartz, especially the best specimens. Beryls are also found in a feldspar vein in gneiss, while at another locality they are found in granite. The celebrated emerald mine of Mount Zebarah, between the river Nile and the Red Sea, mentioned by ancient writers, has lately been reopened. There the gems are found in a black micaceous slate penetrating the granite; they are also found in the granite and in quartz; they are of a pale green colour and full of flaws. Many other localities might be mentioned, but the geological formations are similar.

In New South Wales the emerald and beryl are occasionally found in the tertiary gravels and recent drifts, with other gem stones. They are found *in situ* in the Emmaville district, in association with tinstone, quartz, and other minerals; in the granite at Cooma; associated with mispickel in the Shoalhaven River; and in white feldspar with quartz at Ophir.

The emeralds obtained near Emmaville, and which were placed upon the London market a short time back, are found in a lode formation, associated with quartz, fluorite, topaz, mispickel, tinstone, and kaolin. The lode is rather irregular in width, and in the widest portions large quantities of emeralds are found, often with kaolin. Small stones predominate, and they are light in colour, but some when cut are very brilliant. If they were darker in colour and larger, they would be very valuable. They were selling at about two guineas a carat for cut stones. It seems reasonable to suppose that, when sufficient capital is employed to work this district, large quantities of emeralds will be obtained. Unfortunately the matrix is very hard, the gems often being broken on extraction.

A complete set, in the Museum collection, is exhibited to illustrate the formation from which these emeralds are obtained, their matrix and associated minerals. A few cut stones are also shown.

The previous localities where the emerald and beryl had been found are as follows :—

County Gough.—Elsmore, Kangaroo Flat, Scrubby Gully, the Gulf, Vegetable Creek, Dundee, Mann River, Paradise Creek.

    ,,   Hardinge.—Tingha, Cope's Creek.

    ,,   Wellington.—Bald Hills, Ophir.

    ,,   Selwyn.—Kiandra.

    ,,   Cowley.—Mount Tennant.

    ,,   St. Vincent.—Shoalhaven River.

SPINEL.

Crystalline system—Cubic.

Hardness—8.

Specific gravity—3·5-3·6.

Lustre—Vitreous.

Cleavage—Octahedral.

Composition—Essentially alumina and magnesia, but the latter is often replaced by protoxide of iron, and by lime. MgO, Al_2O_3 if pure, containing magnesia, 28, alumina 72 per cent., but the black specimens contain as much as 20 per cent. of protoxide of iron.

This mineral covers a wide range as regards colour, more in fact than any other precious stone. It is found in many shades of red, blue, green, yellow, brown, black, and sometimes nearly white.

The most marked of these colours give to this mineral its distinctive names, and its varieties, on account of this difference in colour alone, are 'known as follows :—The deep red as *spinel ruby*, the rose-red as *balas ruby*, the violet as *almandine ruby*, the orange-red as *rubicelle*, and the black as *pleonaste*.

The very dark-coloured specimens are of no importance as gem-stones ; it is only the transparent varieties that are of value, and these are often spoken of as precious spinels. The deep red stones often rival the ruby in colour, but they are inferior in " fire " to that gem, owing to the small refractive and dispersive power possessed by the spinel ; and to its absence of pleiochroism may be attributed its deficient brilliancy. Crystallizing in the cubical system, it cannot of course be dichroic ; but in spite of these defects, large quantities are used for jewellery, were originally considered identical with the Oriental ruby, and were credited with possessing the same supernatural powers as that gem. Even now these stones are frequently, either in error or by fraud, passed off as Oriental rubies ; but this is a deception that should be easy of detection, as they are deficient in hardness, and do not show dichrism ; the specific gravity of the ruby is also higher, and the crystalline system different.

Before the composition of the spinel was determined, and before the introduction of the delicate tests we now use to discriminate between gem-stones, there was no distinction made between the spinel and the Oriental ruby, a fact that accounts for the large number of gigantic stones being regarded during the middle ages as rubies, that are only spinels. De Lisle in 1783 is supposed to have been the first to distinguish between these different gem-stones. It is therefore to be supposed that previous to this date these spinels were honestly believed to be what they were represented, and that they were bought and sold in ignorance, and not with desire to defraud. The differences between the varieties of spinel and the corundum gems, are to a casual observer so slight that it is little to be wondered at that early traders in these gems should have been deceived.

The famous spinel in the Royal Crown of England, once thought to have been a ruby, was known to the Black Prince; it came into his possession, and was afterwards worn by Henry V at Agincourt; it is thus of some historic importance, although its intrinsic value has become lessened by its real composition having been discovered. The knowledge that so many of the historic rubies are simply spinels, casts grave doubts as to whether many other large stones still supposed to be rubies are not spinels.

To illustrate the necessity of correct nomenclature in reference to these gems, the recent history of a fine blue spinel is worth repeating. It was an Indian-cut stone, forwarded to London from that country as a sapphire; it was recut in London and sold as a sapphire; it was subsequently found to be a spinel, and was returned by the purchaser to the merchant from whom he bought it. This stone weighed after recutting 25 carats. Mr. Streeter mentions two fine spinels that were exhibited in the London Exhibition of 1862, one of perfect colour and free from flaws weighed 197 carats; when recut in London it weighed 81 carats, and was then a "perfect stone." The other weighed 102½ carats and when recut weighed 72½ carats.

Most of the large spinels come from India, certainly from the East, and one of the finest recorded belonged to the King of Oude; it was of the size of a pigeon's egg, and had great lustre. Besides India, spinels fit for jewellery come from Burmah, Siam, Ceylon, and the United States of America.

The red varieties of the spinel known as "spinel ruby" and "balas ruby" have little to distinguish them; the stones bearing the latter name are inferior in colour and brilliancy to the former, and less like the true ruby. The origin of the term "balas" has become quite a debatable question; many theories have been put forward by different writers, but it is unnecessary to notice them; it is sufficient that the name distinguishes the stone.

The Persians have a tradition that the mines from which these gems are obtained were discovered through the mountain being divided by an earthquake, and that they were mistaken for the true rubies. There are famous mines at Badakhshan in Tartary, where balas rubies are found, and the natives of this district have a superstition that two large stones always lie near each other, and when one is found they most diligently search for the other; and it is stated that, if unable to find it, they will even break the stone found in order to keep up the belief.

The natives of India call the spinel Lal Rumani, and ascribe to it valuable medicinal properties.

Spinels occur embedded in granular limestone, and with calcite in serpentine, gneiss, and allied rocks. It is also found in the cavities of masses ejected from some volcanoes, for instance, the ancient ejected masses of Mount Somma. They also largely occur as water-worn pebbles in the beds of rivers, and alluvial deposits of many localities. A few good stones of small size have been found in California. A pale blue spinel is found in Sweden, embedded in limestone. Green spinels are found in slate in the Ural Mountains. In Bohemia small rose-red crystals occur with pyrites.

Spinel, as has been stated, crystallizes in the cubical system, and its principal form is the octahedron, sometimes showing faces of the rhombic dodecahedron, it is also found as twins, the twinning taking place parallel to one face of the octahedron. Some of the small crystals are so perfect, and of such a good lustre, that they might be used for the purpose of ornamentation in their natural state. Their form of crystallization readily distinguishes them from the ruby; the other differences have already been pointed out.

From garnets, they may be distinguished by being infusible, garnets fusing easily in thin splinters in the blowpipe flame. Both these minerals crystallizing in the cubical system, their optical properties cannot be used to distinguish between them; the inferior hardness of the garnet is also useful in deciding the difference; the specific gravity of both are nearly alike, so that this test cannot be used with any certainty. The difference between spinel and coloured topaz is easily determined by the dichroism of the latter, and by topaz becoming electric when heated, a property not possessed by the spinel; the difference of crystalline form is also useful, and even in waterworn stones there is often a cleavage plane on the topaz sufficient to assist in its determination.

The higher specific gravity of zircon is sufficient to distinguish it from spinel, besides it is less hard, has a different crystalline form, and becomes pale or colourless when heated in the blowpipe flame, while the spinel becomes darker under this test.

The black spinel (pleonaste) might be mistaken for magnetite, but is not magnetic.

The spinel is interesting as having been made artificially very successfully, by heating together alumina, magnesia, and boracic acid at a very high temperature; the latter has the power of dissolving the two other constituents, and volatalising when greatly heated; these spinels were obtained in perfect crystals, and having the correct hardness. Spinel crystals have also been obtained by other methods.

Spinels vary much in price. Small stones range from 5s. to 10s. per carat; medium stones, of fair colour, 20s. to 40s.; large stones, 60s. to 100s. per carat, but they must be of good colour and free from flaws. The balas ruby varies much in price. Good spinels are valuable stones and worth searching for.

In this Colony spinels are sometimes found in alluvial deposits with other gem-stones; they are usually small, and might be easily mistaken for garnets, but on account of the superior value of spinels over the latter stones, it is advisable to be certain as to the identity of red stones, if of any size or of good colour. When spinels are found in a sedimentary deposit, they were originally derived from older rocks. The following are the principal localities from which the spinel has been recorded in New South Wales :—

County Arrawatta—Severn River.
    ,,   Bathurst—Bathurst District.
    ,,   Clarke—Oban.
    ,,   Gough—Yarrow Waterholes.
    ,,   Hardinge—Tingha.
    ,,   Murchison—Bingera.
    ,,   Phillip—Cudgegong River.
    ,,   Sandon—Uralla.

GARNET.

Crystalline system—Cubic.
Hardness—6·5—7·5.
Specific gravity—3·15—4·3.
Lustre—Vitreous to resinous.
Cleavage—Parallel to the faces of the rhombic dodecahedron, sometimes distinct.
Composition—Unisilicates of various sesquioxides and protoxides. The sesquioxides being alumina, iron, or chromium, and sometimes manganese. The protoxides are those of iron, lime, magnesia, or manganese.

C

The following are the principal varieties, with their formulæ, these showing at a glance the replacement of the various bases, to form the different sub-species :—

1. Lime-alumina garnet ... $=6\ CaO,\ 3\ SiO_2 + 2\ Al_2\ O_3,\ 3\ SiO_2$
2. Magnesia-alumina garnet ... $=6\ MgO,\ 3\ SiO_2 + 2\ Al_2\ O_3,\ 3\ SiO_2$
3. Iron-alumina garnet ... $=6\ FeO,\ 3\ SiO_2 + 2\ Al_2\ O_3,\ 3\ SiO_2$
4. Manganese-alumina garnet... $=6\ MnO,\ 3\ SiO_2 + 2\ Al_2\ O_3,\ 3\ SiO_2$
5. Iron-lime garnet ... ... $=6\ CaO,\ 3\ SiO_2 + 2\ Fe_2\ O_3,\ 3\ SiO_2$
6. Lime-chrome garnet ... $=6\ CaO,\ 3\ SiO_2 + 2\ Cr_2\ O_3,\ 3\ SiO_2$

The above may be considered as the types, the composition not being always constant.

The chemical structure of the six kinds is seen to be identical, the replacement being by elements of equal chemical value. The group is a large one, and includes several gem-stones largely used for ornamental purposes. Some of the varieties are very abundant, and this renders them of comparatively little value ; but many of them nevertheless possess many qualities that are necessary in precious stones. They are found of almost every depth of hue and colour, and they also vary much in hardness and specific gravity. They all crystallize in the cubical system, are singly refractive, and not dichroic ; they are usually found crystallized as the rhombic dodecahedron, or as the icositetrahedron, the octahedron being extremely rare.

Besides the property of cubical crystallization, which belongs to the whole group, there is another character common to them all, with the exception of the lime-chrome garnet (ouvarovite), namely, fusibility before the blowpipe. This test alone is sufficient to determine the garnet from many stones much resembling it in colour and other properties ; this has been pointed out previously.

The name garnet is (on the authority of Dana) from the Latin *granatus* (like a grain), because it is usually found in granular forms, although the origin of the name is, by some authorities, traced to its similarity to the seeds of the pomegranate.

The name carbuncle, by which the garnet is often known, is applied in many different ways, and is somewhat misleading ; it at one time denotes the manner of cutting, at other times it is used to distinguish the almandine or iron-alumina garnet. The ancients gave the name to all red stones, while modern writers are certainly not more definite in their use of the word. Theophrastus says it resembles burning coal, and emits light in the dark. The Hebrew for carbuncle is a word meaning lightning, and we are told that the Jews have a legend that this stone was suspended in Noah's Ark to diffuse light. The word is now used to denote the scarlet and deep red garnets, cut *en cabochon*. There is no necessity for the use of the word, and it should be discarded.

The garnet was a favourite stone among the ancients. The Greeks and Romans were extremely fond of this gem, and used it largely for engravings. Several specimens are now to be seen in Paris, Rome, and St. Petersburg. The celebrated Marlborough garnet, engraved with the head of the dog " Sirius," is considered to be a masterpiece of this kind of art. A magnificently engraved stone, contained in the Berlin collection, is a splendid specimen of the Greek school. The Persians were very fond of engraving the portraits of their rulers on this stone. It was largely employed by the Celts and Anglo-Saxons for jewellery, filigree, and enamel work, slabs of polished garnet of considerable area being used by them as inlays.

The common garnet occurs in mica slate, granite, gneiss, limestone, chlorite slate, serpentine, basaltic rocks, &c. It is distributed plentifully all over the world. The Syrian or Oriental garnet is found in alluvial soil in India, Pegu, Ceylon, &c. The Syrian garnets, so-called, do not come from Syria, but take their name from Siriam, a city in Pegu, and a market for the finest stones. They are found from a quarter of an inch to three inches in diameter; they are cut with emery or garnet powder, on a copper wheel, and polished with tripoli powder, on lead. They are usually kept thin on account of their depth of colour.

It will now be advisable to consider each variety of the garnet separately, as they differ so widely from each other in colour, appearance, hardness, specific gravity, value, &c. The order will be that enumerated above.

1. Essonite, or Cinnamon Stone.

The lime-alumina garnet. As the name implies, this is of a pale cinnamon colour, it is the lightest of the Essonite garnets, a darker stone being known as hyacinth, a word which is unfortunate, as it tends to confound this gem with the zircon. Essonite is obtained principally in Ceylon, where it is found in large pieces. It is also found in Scotland, Ireland, and the United States. It is sufficiently hard to just scratch quartz. It is the most easily fusible of all the garnets, and has a specific gravity of 3·5–3·6. It is used to a large extent in jewellery, some fine cut stones being in the Townshend collection. Another lime-alumina garnet, having almost the same composition as essonite, is called *grossularite*. It is of a pale green colour, and was named from the botanical name of the gooseberry, *Ribes grossularia*. It occurs in serpentinous rocks in Siberia. It is also found in Norway.

The approximate composition of essonite is $SiO_2 = 40$, $Al_2 O_3 = 20$, $Fe_2 O_3 = 4$, $CaO = 33$.

Grossularite contains more iron, and less alumina.

2. Pyrope.

Sometimes known as the Bohemian garnet, is the magnesia-alumina variety, and is found in Bohemia, Saxony, and other parts of Germany; also in Ceylon, in alluvial deposits. It is of a blood-red colour, and usually found in rounded or angular fragments; it is rarely found crystallized. It is one of the hardest of the garnets, and has been mistaken for the ruby. When cut as a brilliant, it is a very bright stone, but being found in small pieces, it is usually rose-cut. These stones are greatly esteemed in Austria, Turkey, and other adjoining countries, and fetch high prices. The pyrope always contains a good deal of iron, with some chromium and manganese, these doubtless being the cause of its rich color. The inferior sorts are largely used in the cheap Bohemian jewellery, of which it forms the chief part.

The name pyrope means fire-like. It has a specific gravity of 3·69–3·8; it fuses with difficulty.

Approximate composition :—$SiO_2 = 42$, $Al_2 O_3 = 20$, $Fe_2 O_3 = 2$, $FeO = 9$, $MgO = 10-20$ $CaO = 1-6$ and up to 4 per cent. of $Cr_2 O_3$.

3. Almandine.

Known as precious garnet, and is the iron-alumina garnet. It is the most valued of all the varieties, and is largely used for jewellery. The range of colour lies between a purple-amethyst and a brownish-red. The pure, fiery, scarlet stones are generally cut *en cabochon*, often with a hollow at the back, in which a piece of foil is placed to enhance their brilliancy. This foiling was customary long before the time of Pliny.

This garnet is said to derive the name of "almandine" from Pliny, who applied the term "Alabandicus" to the "carbunculus" cut and polished at Alabanda.

These stones have of late years gone out of fashion, though at one time a good stone of the size of half-a-crown would fetch as much as £50.

Some of these red garnets have been fashioned into cups and boxes. The Mayer collection at Liverpool, England, includes a cup of this material, while another is in the Hope collection. A delicate cross is sometimes seen in these stones, the star having four rays.

The hardness of the almandine garnet is 6·5–7·5, and its specific gravity 3·7–4·21. Its common crystal form is that of the rhombic dodecahedron.

Its approximate composition is $SiO_2=40$, $Al_2 O_3=20$, $FeO=35$, sometimes with some MnO, MgO, and CaO.

The precious garnet is found in Ceylon in alluvial deposits, and also in gneiss; it is also found in India, Brazil, and many other countries.

The common garnet is found all over the world. It is a brownish red, subtranslucent, or opaque variety; its composition is similar to that of the almandine garnet.

4. Spessartite.

The manganese-alumina garnet is named from Spessart, in Bavaria. It is not a plentiful stone, and is not used to any extent in jewellery. It is of a deep hyacinth or brownish-red colour, having a hardness of 7–7·5, with a specific gravity of 3·7–4·4. Its approximate composition is $SiO_2=35$, $Al_2 O_3=14$, $FeO=14$, $MnO=35$.

It is distinguished by its strong manganese reactions, with the proper tests.

5. Andradite (The Iron-lime Garnet).

Several garnets are included under the general name of andradite. They have a hardness above 7, and a specific gravity of 3·44. Their approximate composition is $SiO_2=36$, $Fe_2 O_3=30$, $MnO=3$, $CaO=29$, and usually some potassium.

Aplome, colophonite, pyrenite, a black garnet named melanite, and a transparent yellow or greenish stone named topazolite, are the principal iron-lime garnets; they are little used in jewellery, being perhaps mineralogical curiosities more than commercial articles. At present they are rare.

6. Ouvarovite.

The lime-chrome garnet was named after Uvarof, President of the Imperial Academy, St. Petersburg. This gem has a fine emerald-green colour, but it is unfortunately of rare occurrence. When sufficiently large it is a beautiful stone, having a hardness of 7·5–8 with specific gravity 3·4. It is found in the Ural mountains, associated with chromic iron (chromite). As chromite is common in this Colony it would be well to bear *ouvarovite* in mind. Its approximate composition is $SiO_2=35$, $Al_2 O_3=5$, $Cr_2 O_3=22$, $CaO=30$, with some iron and magnesia. It gives chromium reactions with the borax bead.

Some extremely beautiful but rather soft gems of various hues of green to brownish green, have been imported into England, for use as ornamental stones, since the year 1878. They are found in the gold washings of the river Bobrowsha, in the Urals. They occur in nodular masses, up to one inch in diameter. Their refractive and dispersive powers are high, and the stones exhibit a large amount of "fire." The hardness is about 5, with a specific gravity 3·85. It is yet doubtful whether they belong to the garnet group. They might be mistaken for the green lime-chrome garnet, ouvarovite, although the hardness should be sufficient to distinguish between them.

From the above it will be seen that the name garnet embraces a large number of different gems, having affinities principally in the chemical law governing their composition, and in their constant crystalline form.

The common garnet is supposed to be known to everyone. As a rule we may consider it to belong to the iron-alumina variety, but there is no reason to suppose but that specimens of the other varieties may at some time or other be found in this Colony.

Undoubted specimens of the magnesia-alumina garnet (pyrope) would be of value if found, and good almandine or precious garnets would certainly be worth finding. In a paper read before the Royal Society of N. S. Wales, the author described precious garnets found at Pyrmont, Sydney; they are however very small. The garnets from the M'Donnell Ranges of South Australia (the so-called Australian rubies) are much too dark, and are deficient in "fire," yet with these defects their value as rough uncut stones was in the year 1883 set down as equivalent to 23s. per pound, so that these inferior garnets have some commercial value. One often sees in the jewellers' shops, these gems cut for rings, &c., and labelled as Australian rubies. Although deficient in colour, lustre, and brilliancy to the ruby, yet they are real stones and preferable to paste gems.

Common garnets are so plentifully distributed, that none but the superior kinds are worth consideration from a commercial point of view. In New South Wales garnets are found in many localities, some good crystallized specimens being obtained at Broken Hill; they are also found throughout the Colony, principally at the mining centres. It is unnecessary to enumerate the very large number of New South Wales localities from which the garnet has been recorded.

TOPAZ.

Crystalline system—Rhombic.
Hardness—8.
Specific gravity—3·4-3·6.
Lustre—Vitreous.
Cleavage—Parallel to the basal plane, highly perfect.
Composition—Silicate of alumina, and fluoride of silicon, silica 16 2, silicic fluoride 28·1, alumina 55·7 per cent.

The word topaz is supposed to be derived from Topazion, an island in the Red Sea, as stated by Pliny; but the topaz mentioned by him was not the same stone that we call topaz, as it yielded to the file, and had a hardness less than 7. It was most probably the same gem now known as chrysolite or peridot, because topaz was not known as a distinct stone until comparatively modern times.

The topaz is one of the few precious stones containing fluorine; in fact, the presence of this element is most rare in this class of minerals.

Although the topaz is a distinct mineral species, yet, through a misapplication of terms, other stones are also known as topaz, especially the yellow sapphires known as "Oriental Topaz," and the "occidental" or "Scotch topaz," which is nothing but yellow quartz. The differences between these three stones are easy of determination ; the following figures readily showing this :—

Oriental topaz (yellow sapphire) has hardness 9 and specific gravity about 4.

Brazilian topaz (topaz proper) has hardness 8 and specific gravity about 3·5.

Scotch topaz (quartz) has hardness 7 and specific gravity about 2·65.

It is very necessary to bear in mind that this variety of quartz is spoken of as topaz, because the general appearance of a well cut quartz specimen of this character is likely to deceive one, but the tests necessary to determine the difference between it and real topaz are so easy of application that no one need be imposed upon. Besides the tests noted above, the topaz shows pyro-electricity in a very high degree; of course care must be taken not to heat the stone too rapidly or too strongly, as the perfect basal cleavage of the topaz might, by splitting the stone, destroy a good gem. The physical properties characteristic of gems have already been dealt with.

The double refraction of topaz is strong, and when the specimen is sufficiently coloured, the pleiochroism is very marked ; in almost colourless stones a difference of tint in the two squares can be detected when viewed through the dichroiscope. Some colourless topazes found in Brazil are very brilliant, and show dazzling reflections when properly cut, so much so that those named "Minas Novas," from the locality whence they are obtained, are sometimes sold as diamonds, although the difference in hardness should prevent this. They are also known as "pingas d'agoa," or "gouttes d'eau."

Usually topazes are slightly coloured, and are found in different shades of yellow, blue, pink, red, green, citron, &c. Blue and pale green topazes are found of large size, and are often more brilliant than specimens of beryl having similar colours. The polish, too, that the topaz takes is very brilliant.

The sherry-coloured and the brownish-tinted specimens from some localities can be made of a pink hue by heating them at a moderate temperature. The beautiful pink colour thus obtained is rarely seen in natural specimens. The action of sunlight has great influence on the colouring matter of the wine-coloured topaz, so much so that the beautiful collection of Russian topaz crystals in the British (Natural History) Museum, is kept shrouded from the light of day. What the cause of this change of colour is remains to be decided ; but evidence points to a change in the molecular arrangement, rather than to the presence of impurities.

Some large topazes have been found in different localities, although it is rarely that large stones are without defects. Specimens of great size, and finely crystallized, are found in the Ural Mountains. One specimen from this locality (in the collection at St. Petersburg) is perfectly transparent, is of a wine colour, weighs 31 lbs., and is 4¾ inches long and 4¼ inches wide. One specimen found in Scotland weighed 19 ounces. It may be as well to mention here that the topaz is one of the very few gems found in the British Islands. It is found in good quantity in the Cairngorm Mountains in Scotland, together with the quartz specimens known as Scotch topaz. In the London Exhibition of 1862 some large specimens were shown from this locality, sent as pebbles. These were considered by the people living in the locality to be quartz pebbles, and no doubt many a fine gem has been thrown away under that impression. The following will serve to illustrate the advantage of being able to determine these gems : A large mass of white topaz, now in the British Museum collection, was at one time used as a door-stop by a marine store dealer in London. He sold it for 3s. It weighs 12 lb. avoirdupois.

It has been stated that the topazes taken from the beds of the rivers at Capao, in Brazil, secured a net profit of £3,000 in twelve years.

At present the commercial value of the topaz is small. A stone of good size and of good colour may be purchased for a pound or two, while smaller stones, in the rough, are only worth a few shillings per pound avoirdupois ; still they are of some value, and worthy of collection, especially in the New England District of New South Wales, where they are plentifully distributed. Good pink stones (which, of course, are manufactured from topazes having a suitable colour) are worth from about £2 per ounce. In some parts of India the topaz is of far greater value than in England.

Tavernier describes a topaz, weighing 157 carats, belonging to the Emperor Aurungzeb, an Indian monarch, which had been purchased by him for the large sum of £18,000. This might have been an " Oriental topaz."

Formerly these gems were of far more value, but fashions change and tastes differ ; and gem stones, being used principally for ornamental purposes, are entirely at the mercy of fickle fancy.

The topaz has been occasionally used by the engraver, even from very early times, intaglios being in existence of early Greek workmanship. An antique engraving, bearing a cluster of stars, in the St. Petersburg collection ; the portraits of Phillip II. and Don Carlos, engraved on a topaz, in the Royal Library of Paris ; and the engraved seal ring owned by the Emperor Hadrian, are among the few engraved specimens of this gem. It does not appear to have been generally in favour for work of this class.

Topaz is cut on a leaden wheel with emery, and polished with tripoli powder. The best form of cutting is as a " brilliant " having the table smaller than in the diamond. The large so-called diamond in the Portuguese Treasury is supposed to be a topaz ; it is as large as a hen's egg.

The topaz is found in almost every part of the world, and in Saxony constitutes massive rocks, known as " topaz fels." Often this gem is associated with granite and gneiss, and usually some fluorine is contained in these rocks. In the Urals it is found in granite. In Brazil it is found in a loose sandy clay. Some beautiful blue specimens have been found in Colorado, in the United States ; pale violet in Saxony ; sea-green, sometimes known as aquamarine, in Bohemia ; blue in Scotland ; while Brazilian specimens are found of nearly all colours.

The topaz is, when crystallized, found as rhombic prisms, usually having but one end regularly terminated. When thus seen it cannot be mistaken for quartz, which crystallizes in the hexagonal system ; nor for the yellow sapphire, which is also hexagonal. This difference in crystalline form, together with the perfect basal cleavage of topaz, and difference in hardness, are usually quite sufficient to determine the topaz ; even in waterworn pebbles a flat portion is usually seen where the topaz has cleaved.

Very fine topazes occur in the southern portion of the Urals, in the Ilmen Hills. They are also found in the Mourzinsk deposits in the north-east of Ekaterinburg. The largest topaz known was found here. It is now in the museum of the Mining Institute. It measures 27 centimetres (about 10½ inches) in length, and 31 centimetres (about 12 inches) in circumference.

The topaz is common in New South Wales, especially in localities where tin is obtained, and specimens have been found of large size, especially those from near Mudgee.

The following are the localities in New South Wales from which the topaz has been obtained :—

County Bathurst—Bathurst District.
　　　　,,　　Clarendon—Gundagai District.
　　　　,,　　Clarke—Oban.
　　　　,,　　Georgiana—Abercrombie River.
　　　　,,　　Gough—Dundee, Glen Creek, Inverell, Pond's Creek, Scrubby
　　　　　　　　Gully, Vegetable Creek.
　　　　,,　　Hardinge—Balola, Cope's Creek.
　　　　,,　　Inglis—Tamworth.
　　　　,,　　Murchison—Bingera.
　　　　,,　　Phillip—Cooyal, Cudgegong River, Gulgoug, Two-mile Flat,
　　　　　　　　near Mudgee.
　　　　,,　　Wellington—Bell River.
　　　　,,　　Sandon—Uralla.

Professor David, referring to the Vegetable Creek tinfields, states that "The topaz is very abundant in the alluvials of most of the creeks which drain from the Mole table-land. It would appear from this that the intrusive tin granite is the original matrix of the gem, though it has not yet been found here *in situ*. At Scrubby Gully topazes of a pale sky-blue colour are to be found in great abundance. White topazes are plentiful at Blather Arm Creek."

Simple forms of the Rhombic System.

As crystallized specimens of topaz are so different in form from those of quartz or yellow sapphire, it will be well to describe, as simply as possible, the most distinctive forms belonging to this system.

The basis of the system is that of three axes, *all of unequal lengths*, and all at right angles. Either one of these axes (which may be either longer or shorter than the others), may be taken for the principal or vertical axis, and when this is chosen, the longer of the other two is known as the *macro-diagonal*, and the shorter as the *brachy-diagonal*.

The right rhombic pyramid is bounded by eight scalene triangles, the axes join the solid angles, so that the base of each pyramid is rhombic in form ; it may be considered as composed of two rhombic pyramids placed base to base.

The right rectangular pyramid.—When the lateral axes join the central points of the lateral edges, the base of the pyramid is rectangular in form ; it is bounded by eight isosceles triangles, four of which are larger than the other four.

The right rhombic prism is closed at the ends by equal rhombs, and it has four rectangular faces forming the sides of the prism. Instead of a rhomb, the prism may be terminated by combinations of the pyramidal faces. This is a form the topaz takes.

The right rectangular prism has the ends closed by equal rectangles, because the lateral axes meet the centres of the rectangles that form the prism, instead of the upright edges, as in the rhombic prism. It is bounded by six rectangular faces, opposite pairs of which are equal to each other.

There are other forms (and some crystals belonging to this system are very complicated), but in this simple description it will be unnecessary to notice them, with the exception of the hemihedral form of the right rhombic pyramid ; this is called the *rhombic sphenoid*, and is derived from the holohedral form, by the development of each alternate face, to the exclusion of the remainder. The figure is bounded by four scalene triangular faces, and somewhat resembles a wedge.

RHOMBIC SYSTEM.
Simple forms.

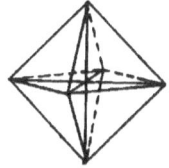

*Right Rhombic
Pyramid.*

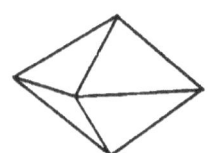

*Right Rectangular
Pyramid.*

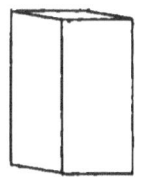

*Right Rhombic
Prism.*

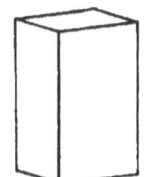

*Right Rectangular
Prism.*

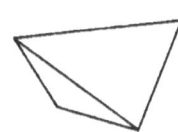

*Right Rhombic
Spheroid.*

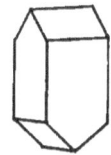

*Combination
Crystal.*

(5 c 201-95-5.)

ZIRCON.

Crystalline System—Tetragonal.
Hardness—7·5.
Specific gravity—4·7–4·8.
Lustre—Adamantine.
Cleavage—Parallel to faces of the prism, indistinct in most instances.
Composition—Silicate of zirconia, $ZrO_2 \; SiO_2$. Silica, 33 ; zirconia, 67 per
cent.

There are several varieties of this gem known by special names, as
"hyacinth," which is red and transparent. "Jargoons," or "jargons," are
colourless or smoky-tinted zircons, (these were so named in allusion· to the
fact that while resembling the diamond in lustre they were, in comparison
with that gem, almost worthless). The zircon or zirconite is grey or brown,
and in some specimens almost opaque. The name is from the Arabic, *zirk*,
meaning a precious stone. Besides these well-defined varieties, the diversity
of colour in this gem is very great, ranging from red to brown, from yellow
to orange, and from blue to green.

This stone forms a very fine gem, and when of a ruby colour might be
mistaken for the spinel ruby, although the higher specific gravity of the
zircon would at once decide the question. When the coloured stones are
heated, they become quite colourless in most instances, thus differing from
either the spinel or the garnet. They do not fuse in the flame of the blow-
pipe, which is a characteristic difference from the garnet. The crystalline
form at once determines the zircon from those stones resembling it in some
of its characters.

The perfectly transparent stones have a lustre almost approaching that
of the diamond, and to this may be attributed the indifference with which
these gem-stones are now treated. They have been used for the purpose of
fraud, having been set in massive gold rings, pawned as brilliants, and of
course never redeemed. A file will not touch them, so that this test for
"paste" fails in this case. The high dispersive power which the zircon has,
also assists to render the determination, by general appearances, deceptive,
but the test of hardness would at once decide the matter, as the zircon is
scratched by topaz, and this is only 8 in the scale.

Were it not for its deceptive characters, its natural properties place it,
for ornamental purposes, next to the diamond. There is a variety obtained
at Matura, Ceylon, which is known as the "Matura diamond". It is often
sold in the bazaars of India for the genuine diamond.

Some of the red specimens are remarkable for the vividness of their tints,
which have been likened to flames of fire ; but with all these good characteristics to recommend them, these gems are not favourites, and fashion
counts for a great deal.

Of course, like all gems, it has been endowed with supernatural properties,
especially during the middle ages. It was considered to have the power to
bring sleep, riches, honor, and wisdom ; to drive away the plague, and to
protect the wearer from evil spirits. We look back with amusement at
the superstitious reverence given to these precious stones in those times,
but to-day the superstition in reference to some gems still remains,
although, perhaps, in a lesser degree. That some precious stones have the
power to bring ill-luck, and that their possession brings disaster and ruin,
is firmly believed by many. One of the minor industries of Australia
suffers at the present time from the effect of this lingering superstition.

At the present time the varieties of the zircon are of little value, being rarely employed in jewellery. Formerly it commanded a very high price, and deservedly so. There is a splendid specimen of an ancient engraved zircon in the Paris Museum, the workmanship being of the best. It is 2 inches in length, and 1¼ inch in width. It represents Moses with the two tables of the law. Lord Duncannon had in his collection a zircon engraved with the figure of an athlete. A very fine gem of the variety hyacinth, is a cameo representing the head of an angel, by Raphael, which was set in a ring, and worn by Gregory XIII. It was engraved with his name. At the back of the cameo the name of Pius VII appears. Ancient intagli are found cut from this stone, and it was largely used by them as engraved signet rings. Down to the last century the "jargoon" was much used in mourning ornaments, and was then considered to be an inferior diamond.

Mr. Streeter says that he has in his collection a green zircon weighing 4½ carats, having the lustre of the diamond, and surpassing the emerald in colour.

Zircons are cut for ornaments, by grinding on a leaden plate with emery powder, and polishing on a copper plate with powdered rotton-stone. The "jargoon" is commonly cut in the form of a rose-diamond or as a brilliant; the "hyacinth" is cut like a brilliant with a rounded table.

The zircon occurs in granite and syenite, also in crystalline limestones, gneiss, chlorite schist, and other metamorphic rocks; it is sometimes found in volcanic rocks, and also in beds of iron-ore. It is also found in alluvial deposits with other gem-stones, and in auriferous sands in many parts. Its characteristic features are its crystalline form (the tetragonal prism often terminated at both ends by the tetragonal pyramid), its high specific gravity, and the property the coloured specimens have of becoming colourless or almost so when highly heated.

In the Townshend collection at the South Kensington Museum are twenty-five cut specimens of the different varieties of the zircon, some of which are very fine stones. Several were obtained near Mudgee, in this Colony, one of which is classed as being a true "hyacinth." Among the collection are zircons of a variety of colours—green, brown, orange, lavender, &c.

In New South Wales zircons are common in the auriferous river sands and drifts. They are, of course, when thus found, more or less rolled. They are found in granite on the Mitta Mitta and on the Moama River, some 4 miles west of Jillamalong Hill, county Cadell. Also in the granite on which Kiandra is built. In the tin country they are very common, and the "green tin" or "brass filings" is composed of minute zircons. This is the gem-sand of the "grave-yard lead" in the New England District.

The following are the principal localities in New South Wales where the zircon has been found :—

County Camden—Berrima, Wingecarribee River.
    ,,   Georgiana—Abercrombie River.
    ,,   Gough—Near Emmaville, Scrubby Gully, Swanbrook, Yarrow Waterholes.
    ,,   Hardinge—Rocky River.
    ,,   Inglis—Tamworth.
    ,,   Murchison—Bingera.
    ,,   Northumberland—Wollombi River.
    ,,   Parry—Bowling Alley Point, Mount Misery, Nundle.
    ,,   Phillip—Cudgegong River.
    ,,   Sandon—Mount James, Uralla.
    ,,   St. Vincent—Shoalhaven River.

TETRAGONAL SYSTEM.
Simple forms.

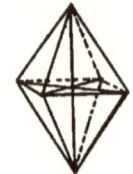

Tetragonal Pyramid.

Ditetragonal Pyramid.

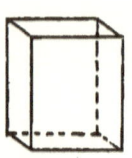

Tetragonal Prism.

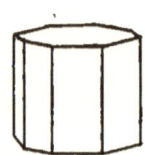

Ditetragonal Prism.

Tetragonal Sphenoid.

Tetragonal Scalenohedron.

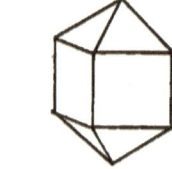

Combination Crystals.

(5 c 201-95-6.)

Simple Forms of the Tetragonal System.

When the zircon is found crystallized it can hardly be mistaken for any other gem, as it crystallizes in this system.

In this system there are three axes, two of which are equal in length, the other may be either longer or shorter than these, this is the vertical or principal axis, the two equal ones are the lateral. All three axes are at right angles to each other.

Tetragonal pyramid.—This figure is bounded by eight isosceles triangles, these being more obtuse or acute as the principal axis is shorter or longer. The base of the pyramid is a square, and the figure is a combination of two of these pyramids as in the octahedron. In the holohedral forms there are two sets of figures depending on the position of the lateral axes; in the first they join the solid tetragonal angles, in the other, the centre of the lateral edges. It is easily seen that, if the faces of both these are developed in the same crystal, we have eight angles, and our crystal will have become a *ditetragonal pyramid*—which figure is bounded by sixteen isosceles triangles, the base of the pyramids being octagonal.

Tetragonal prism.—This form is bounded by four equal rectangles, having two square basal planes to close the figure. There are also two forms in this, as in the pyramid, based upon the position of the lateral axes; in one they join the centre of the rectangles, in the other the vertical edges. This is a common form of the zircon, but the figure is usually surmounted by pyramids instead of the basal planes. If faces of both orders are developed in the same crystal we obtain a *ditetragonal prism*—which figure is bounded by eight rectangular planes, and the basal plane will, of course, be octagonal.

There are two hemihedral forms, the *tetragonal sphenoid*, having four faces formed from the tetragonal pyramid by the development of alternate faces, and the *tetragonal scalenohedron*, having eight faces formed by the development of vertical alternate pairs of faces of the ditetragonal pyramid. These two forms are rarely met with except in combinations.

CHRYSOBERYL.

Crystalline system—Rhombic.
Hardness −8·5.
Specific gravity—3·5—3·84.
Lustre—Vitreous.
Cleavage—Parallel to the brachydome, less distinct parallel to the brachypinakoid.
Composition—Alumina and Glucina (Beryllia), BeO, Al_2O_3=Alumina 80·2, Glucina 19·8 per cent.

This gem has several varieties, known by characteristic names; as the *cymophane*, which embraces the true cat's-eye, the *Alexandrite*, named after the Emperor of Russia, and the hard specimens called "Oriental chrysolite" by jewellers; these are all chrysoberyls, and although differing in hue and physical appearance from each other, contain no essential differences in composition. The hardness of chrysoberyl, together with its lustre and brilliancy, make it a desirable stone for ornamental purposes, as it has a hardness nearly equal to the sapphire, and its brilliancy approaches that of the diamond. It has a good range of colour, but the yellow and greenish-yellow specimens predominate, although white stones are occasionally found.

The variety *Alexandrite* is a dark-green by daylight, but changes to a rasp-berry-red hue by artificial light; this change of colour affords a good illustration of dichroism. By a system of twinning, this variety presents the appearance of an obtuse hexagonal pyramid. Some very fine specimens of alexandrite, free from flaws, and of large size, have been at different times sent to Europe from Ceylon, weighing in some instances as much as 60 carats. Its discovery in the Urals is of recent date, although the original stone came from that locality.

The name *Cymophane*, meaning to appear like a wave of light, is given to those specimens of chrysoberyl that appear to enclose rays of light, a phenomenon no doubt the result of internal reflections. Some good specimens of this variety are in the collection at South Kensington Museum.

The most valuable variety of the chrysoberyl, however, is the *cat's-eye* (also known as cymophane), a rare gem, and not to be confounded with the quartz "cat's-eye," a stone of little commercial value. It is distinguished by its remarkable appearance when a ray of light acts upon it in certain directions. This gem is generally cut *en cabochon*, and when well polished shows a line like a silver wire; these lines are supposed to be caused by the minute internal striations of the crystals. It was called in ancient times " oculus solis "; this eye of the sun is at the present time a favourite in China, and commands a high price there. In India it is greatly prized on account of its supposed power against witchcraft, and it has been stated that this stone is the last that a Cingalese will part with. In India the value rises as the bright lines increase in number; these lines of light are there called " betas."

The colour of some of these stones is quite dark, the fancy colour in America being almost black; the white lines show more distinctly when the ground colour is dark. This gem has become more fashionable of late years, especially in America.

In perfectly cut stones the line should run evenly from end to end, and be in the middle of the stone, should be well defined, not broad, and the ground colour sufficiently dark to contrast well with the line.

The value of good "cat's eyes" appears to be changeable, specimens of good quality, fit for rings, being valued at from £10 to £100, and Mr. Streeter states that several large specimens are on the market worth upwards of £1,000 each.

The value and importance of good specimens of the true "cat's-eyes" or chrysoberyl, and the small value of the quartz "cat's-eye," make it necessary that the distinguishing characteristics should be well marked. The hardness of the quartz variety is only 7, and the specific gravity is but 2·6, so that the determination is easy; besides the ray of light in the quartz is dull, while that of the true "cat's-eye" is iridescent, and the difference in brilliancy is quite marked, the quartz variety being quite dull in comparison. A large specimen of the true "cat's-eye," measuring 5 inches in length, is in the Vienna collection.

A very fine specimen from the Hope collection is in the British Museum.

There is a fibrous variety of quartz that has been of late years found in South Africa; it has been obtained of large size, but specimens of this stone are not likely to be mistaken for the true "cat's-eye," so that it will be unnecessary to consider it here. The most common mistake is that the chrysoberyl is frequently called chrysolite, and mistaken for that gem, but the hardness of chrysolite is but little more than six, and its specific gravity is also less than that of the chrysoberyl.

The transparent yellow chrysoberyl when cut as a "brilliant" might be mistaken for a yellow diamond, although the test of hardness would easily distinguish the latter gem. The difference between the chrysoberyl and the yellow topaz is easily determined, as the topaz becomes electric when heated, while the chrysoberyl does not develop pyro-electricity. The basal cleavage of the topaz will also assist in the determination, if present.

The chrysoberyl is cut on a copper wheel with emery, and polished with Tripoli powder.

The chrysoberyl is found as rolled pebbles in the alluvial deposits in Ceylon, Brazil, and Moravia. It is found embedded in mica slate in the Ural Mountains ; it has been found in granite in the United States of America, and has also been found in Ireland.

It is doubtful whether this gem has yet been discovered in New South Wales; it has been stated, however, that a fragment was found in the Macquarie River. There is no reason why this gem should not exist in the Colony.

CHRYSOLITE.

Crystalline system—Rhombic.
Hardness—6—7.
Specific gravity—3·3—3·5.
Lustre—Vitreous.
Cleavage—Parallel to the brachypinakoid.
Composition—Silicate of Magnesia and Protoxide of Iron $(MgO, FeO)_2$ $Si O_2$. The ratio of iron to magnesia is not constant.

This gem is often mistaken for the chrysoberyl, but differs widely from it in composition and other characteristics, as fully stated under that stone.

The *chrysolite* is the "golden stone" of the ancients, and was at one time considered of very great value, more so even than the diamond.

In the eleventh century we find Marbodus, Bishop of Rennes, in a poem called "Lapidarium," writing of it as follows :—

"The golden Chrysolite a fiery blaze
Mixed with the hues of ocean's green displays."

This proves that the term "golden" was applied to this stone through many centuries.

It was in ancient times much used for ornamental purposes, especially by the ladies ; but it has become of far less importance during late years, although the demand for it revived some years ago, and it was then much used ; but at the present time its value is but small, fine specimens being bought for a few shillings per carat.

The chrysolite is known as *peridot* when of a deep olive-green colour, and *olivine* when yellowish-green. The finest specimens of chrysolite resemble the emerald in colour, and the colour fixes the value of the stone ; the darker the green the higher the price.

Unfortunately the hardness is low, and the stone is readily scratched and dulled by wear, a circumstance perhaps of sufficient importance to account for its depreciation as an ornamental gem-stone.

The chrysolite is electric by friction, but does not develop pyro-electricity, a circumstance sufficiently distinct to determine it from green tourmaline, which it somewhat resembles.

It is supposed to have been the topaz of early writers, but its identification has always been uncertain, and is so at the present day. It is supposed to have been the chrysoberyl of Werner, and the cymophane of Haüy, and has also been connected with the beryl and other gems; but at present the chrysolite, peridot, and olivine are identical, only differing in colour.

The Romans considered this gem of greater importance than most other precious stones, as they set it transparent, considering it to have sufficient brilliancy unaided; most other gems they foiled with gold or copper. They also used it for engraving. Two intagli are in existence, one engraved with the head of Minerva, the other with that of Medusa.

The chrysolite takes a very fine polish, but it is stated to be difficult of attainment. A copper wheel is used for the cutting, and the polishing is done with Tripoli powder and oil. It is cut as a rose diamond, or sometimes "step cut;" occasionally it is cut *en cabochon*. The gem is dichroic, giving squares, one of a green colour, the other straw-yellow.

The chrysolite is essentially a volcanic mineral, commercial stones being found in Egypt, Turkey, Africa, Australia, France, &c.; in fact it may be sought for in any volcanic region. From a scientific point of view its presence in lavas and other igneous rocks, and the discovery of olivine in meteorites, opens up a large field for consideration and investigation. The chrysolite is commonly disseminated in basalt and lavas in grains, although at times it is found as large as a turkey's egg. Large, well-defined crystals are very uncommon.

There are some good specimens of the peridot in the British Museum, and in the Museum of Practical Geology, London. The best peridots obtained during the middle ages retain their superiority at the present time, no finer specimens having been discovered. The best peridots come from Ceylon, Pegu, and Brazil. The word peridot in Oriental language signifies a gem.

Transparent bright-green chrysolites are fairly common in many of the auriferous drifts of the Colony. It has been found in the Shoalhaven and Hunter Rivers, also in some of the creeks that fall into the Cudgegong, county Phillip; at Bingera, the Barrier Range, and at Nundle; in a trap dyke on the Upper Murray, and in basalt at Inverell, and many other places.

OPAL.

Crystalline system—None.
Hardness—5·5–6·5.
Specific gravity—2·21.
Lustre—sub-vitreous, mostly inclining to resinous.
Composition—Essentially silica, SiO_2 + water; differing from quartz (rock crystal) in the following particulars: it contains water, and is not crystalline. Although containing water, in some instances up to 12 per cent., the whole of this water does not appear to be necessary, as a portion may be driven off without injury to the stone.

When we speak of opal as a gem-stone, it does not necessarily follow that all kinds of opal are fit for the purposes of ornamentation, or that opal of any character has a marketable value. It is as well to bear in mind that only the variety known as the "Precious Opal" is of real commercial importance. Of course there are in this variety, as in all other gems, different degrees of quality, based on the characteristic play of colours which distinguishes this very valuable gem. These beautiful colours, often as pure as those of the rainbow, are supposed to be the result of physical structure, and are not caused by the presence of any colouring matter, or of any foreign constituent. They are formed by the decomposition of light, by a multitude of fissures, the sides of which are minutely striated; the whole effect is purely a physical one, and as interesting as the stone is beautiful, its very imperfections being the cause of its remarkable beauty.

The consideration of the other varieties is purely a mineralogical matter, and not of sufficient importance to be fully described here. But the enumeration of them is necessary to prevent misunderstanding, and to enable one to decide what Precious Opal really is. They will be listed and described presently. Although necessary to be represented in a mineralogical collection, it is not worth while to trouble about them except from a scientific point of view, as they are of little commercial importance. I mention this matter, because it has come under my own observation, that people living in the country, led away by the broad term "Opal," have gone to great trouble over quite worthless specimens. It is often difficult to make them understand that, although an opal, their specimen is a valueless one.

The precious opal, distinguished by its play of colours, is perhaps, one of the most beautiful ornamental stones in existence, and has always been regarded as one of the most attractive for personal adornment; but like most other gems it has suffered from the effects of fashion, and perhaps, more than any other, from the prevalence of superstition.

Where, when, or how the idea first arose that the possession of an opal brought ill luck, and to the wearer certain disaster, cannot now be decided; but the fact remains that to-day many people cannot be persuaded to wear one, however beautiful or costly it might be. Of course, educated people would laugh at the idea, and consider themselves above popular superstitions, yet it is well known that the opal trade has suffered severely from the effect of this superstition. Poor people, as a rule, do not wear precious stones, and those who wear expensive jewellery are not often illiterate. It is a fact, too, that those who have purchased opals have, in some instances, asked to have them changed for some other gem, because "their pets have died," or "their children have been sick," or "nothing but bad luck has come to them since possessing the opal;" they would, they say, rather wear some other stone.

This prejudice is the more remarkable, because in the mediæval times opals were thought to bestow every possible good, and even as late as the seventeenth century this good opinion prevailed.

The first recorded instance of ill luck following the possession of an opal is that mentioned by Pliny, when relating the story of Nonius, a Roman senator, who possessed a magnificent opal valued at about £20,000 of our money. Mark Antony saw the gem and wished to purchase it; Nonius declined to part with it, and for this was outlawed and sent into exile. Its possession in this instance certainly brought ill luck to Nonius, but Mark Antony had little reason afterwards to boast of his good luck.

The bad reputation of the opal was much intensified by Sir Walter Scott in the Waverley novels. I would refer anyone interested to Rudolph's narrative in Anne of Geierstein, chapters ten and eleven, and no doubt the powerful writings of the author of these novels, had great influence with the public of his day. The opal in this tale was said to reflect all the emotions of the wearer in a most marked manner, and when at last the dreaded drop of holy water alighted upon the stone, it shot out one vivid flash of light, became dull and colourless as an ordinary stone; and the earthly life of the beautiful lady was closed.

During the prevalence of a plague at Venice, at a time when the opal was much worn, the attendants at the hospitals declared that before the death of the victim the opal upon his finger would brighten and glow. It is not difficult to understand the rapid spread a statement of this character would make at such a time, and no scientific explanation would be sufficient to remove the impression that this fatal gem foretold the death of its owner, even if it did not prevent his recovery. It is well known that the precious opal is very sensitive to the influence of heat, and a jeweller will hold in his hand for a short time a specimen he is about to show a customer; the heat from his hand being sufficient to improve the appearance of the gem. Even the increase of temperature of a warm day is sufficient to make a marked improvement in the opal.

It is to be hoped, however, that the ill repute of the opal will go the way of all superstitions, and the day is not far distant when this gem will again take its proper place among precious stones. Her Majesty the Queen of England has done much to break down this prejudice, the opal being a favourite stone with her; and many members of the royal houses in Europe, and also of the aristocracy, are now becoming purchasers of the opal. Already (1893) opals are becoming fashionable in Europe.

The principal supply of precious opal, before its discovery in Australia, came from Hungary, where it is found in a claystone porphyry, in a mountain range near Czernowitz. It is also found in the province of Gracias, Honduras, and although less fiery than the Hungarian specimens, the conditions of occurrence of the American opal, are similar to those of its European rival. A specimen from Honduras, weighing 602 carats, and valued at £5,000, was exhibited at the Centennial Exhibition at Philadelphia in 1876.

The Hungarian mines were discovered in the fifteenth century, and although from that time a very large quantity of opal has been taken from the mines (which are skilfully worked), they still produce fine specimens. Two very large opals were found there in 1863, and exhibited at the Paris Exhibition in 1867; one weighed 186 carats, the other 160 carats; the latter is said to be the finest gem of its class ever seen.

The Queensland opals occur principally in the Gregory South District, in the south-western portion of the Colony, being found in the M'Gregor, Coleman, Grey, and Canaway Ranges, where it occurs in ferruginous siliceous ironstone nodules, or in a "bandstone" underlying the sandstone. The opal-bearing rock is obtained where possible by removing the overlying sandstone. When the amount of material to be removed becomes too great, "driving" is resorted to, in the clay or cement "bottom" underlying the opal-bearing bandstone. A collection of photographs, showing this opal country, and the modes of working to obtain the opal in this part of Queensland, is exhibited in the Museum. I had the pleasure of inspecting a large consignment of these opals which had arrived from Queensland. There were some hundred weights of matrix and opal, presenting a very beautiful appearance. Some of the specimens were large, and from which good gems could be cut, but a very large quantity consisted of thin veins in the brown ferruginous matrix, these being only fit for cameos, for which they are particularly suited, the brilliant colours of the gem forming a marked contrast to the dark background of the matrix.

During the last few years beautiful opal has been found in this Colony, at a locality known as White Cliffs. This field is situated in the county of Yungnulgra, on the Momba Run, about 60 miles in a north-westerly direction from Wilcannia. In the year 1889, a hunter found a piece of precious opal of good quality, and by careful search the opal was discovered *in situ.* In 1890 several mineral leases were applied for, and since that time a large quantity of opals have been obtained there. In 1892 one leaseholder raised about 500 oz. of precious opal, valued at over £2,000. Some of the opal from this field has realised as much as £18 per oz. In the early part of 1893 about twenty miners were working the various properties with a fair amount of success. During that year mining for opal was so successful that a township sprang up, the population being estimated at about 700 persons. The sum realised from the sale of the opal raised during 1893 at this locality was £17,000, some very fine stones being obtained. The opal is found at an average depth of from 10 to 12 feet from the surface, although in some instances it has been obtained at a greater depth. Mr. Pittman, the Government Geologist, believes that the opal will be found at greater depths. The surface is a red clay, beneath this is a layer of gypsum, and then about 2 feet of hard sandstone, below this the opal-bearing rock is found. The ground is also worked when possible by open-cuttings.

Fossil remains are found here altered into precious opal.

There appears to be little doubt that opals exist plentifully over this portion of the Colony, and eventually when the demand for these gems shall have increased, a good trade will be done, and perhaps a profitable industry be established. Large areas of opal country are as yet untouched, although much opal was recovered during the year 1894.

Among the large historical specimens of the opal may be mentioned the one at Vienna, found in 1770, at Czernowitz; it weighs 17 oz., and although having many defects, it is stated that the sum of £10,000 has been refused for it.

Perhaps the most remarkable opal ever recorded was the one owned by the Empress Josephine; this was known as the "Burning of Troy," because of the red flames on its surface, giving it the appearance of being on fire. The under side of this gem was opaque, a peculiarity often observed in the Honduras opal; the upper portion was transparent, through which the fiery rays were seen.

There were some very valuable opals in the Hope collection; one engraved with the head of Apollo is supposed to be of great antiquity.

The opal is cut upon a leaden wheel with emery, and polished on a wooden wheel with tripoli powder and water, and lastly with felt. Great care has to be taken not to heat the stone too much by friction. They are cut *en cabochon*, both sides often being convex.

It is a difficult matter to engrave opals, on account of their brittle nature, but some fine engraved specimens are in existence.

Unfortunately the opal is, for a precious stone, low in the scale of hardness, and is not desirable for rings on that account; but it is largely used for bracelets, pendants, and ornaments for the head. It is very liable to be injured by contact with oily or greasy substances.

The value of the precious opal depends entirely upon its brilliancy and play of colours. The prices given by Mr. Streeter are as follows:—

> The smallest stones, £1 to £1 10s. per carat.
> medium stones, £2 to £3   „
> larger stones, £3 to £5   „

Specimens of good size and purity, on account of their extreme rarity, are very valuable.

D

The opal has a conchoidal fracture, is infusible before the blowpipe, but when thus heated gives off water and becomes opaque. When the precious opal shows patches of every hue, it is known by jewellers as "harlequin opal."

One or other of the several varieties, of the opal are found all over the Colony of New South Wales, but the precious opal is rare. It has, however, been found, besides White Cliffs, at the following localities :—Rocky Bridge Creek, Abercrombie River, county Georgiana; in amygdaloidal basalt at Trunkey; in clay ironstone in the Wellington district; at Louisa Creek; at Bland near Forbes; at Coroo; and at Bloomfield near Orange.

The other varieties of the opal are as follows :—

1. Fire Opal.

Shows yellowish and reddish colours, and when turned to the light appears to give fire-like reflections; it is common in Mexico.

2. Common Opal.

Is semi-opaque, usually of one colour, greenish or yellowish, and translucent. This is much used in Germany for cheap jewellery, and to ornament canes, boxes, and such like articles.

3. Resin Opal.

Is waxy or resinous in appearance, and usually of a yellowish colour.

4. Wood Opal.

Is a variety where the tissues of wood have been replaced by hydrous silica, often so perfectly as to show distinctly the concentric rings of the tree. This is therefore a pseudomorph; it is readily scratched by a knife, thus differing from silicified wood.

5. Agate Opal.

Is composed of opal having different shades of colour, and a structure like agate.

6. Menilite or Liver Opal.

Is an opaque liver-coloured variety.

7. Hydrophane.

Is an opaque, white, or yellowish variety, adheres to the tongue and becomes translucent, or often transparent when placed in water, hence the name.

8. Hyalite.

Is a perfectly transparent, colourless variety, resembling glass, and is often known as "Muller's glass."

Besides these we have *siliceous sinter* and *geyserite*, and other varieties of this class of hydrous silica.

TURQUOIS.

Crystalline System—None, usually reniform, stalactitic, or incrusting.
Hardness—6.
Specific gravity—2·6–2·8.
Lustre—Inclining to waxy, feeble.
Composition—Hydrous phosphate of alumina, with a few per cent. of protoxide of copper. Al_2O_3, P_2O_5+5 H_2O.

Tubal : " One of them showed me a ring that he had of your daughter for a monkey."
Shylock : " Out, upon her! Thou torturest me, Tubal : it was my turquois; I had it of Leah when I was a bachelor. I would not have given it for a wilderness of monkeys."
—*Merchant of Venice*, Act III, Scene 1.

This precious stone acquired its name from having been imported into Europe by way of Turkey.

The turquois of commerce comes from Khorassan, in Persia, and it still maintains its superiority, although the gem has been found in a great many other localities, especially Mexico. In Persia it occurs in a mountainous district, and is found in clay slate in veins traversing the mountain in all directions. The best specimens from this locality are noted for the delicate hue of the blue tinged with green, and the faint translucency which they possess. The Shah of Persia has in his possession some very fine turquoises, and he is accredited with taking for himself all the finest specimens found in his dominions, the inferior alone being permitted to leave the country.

These gems are found in varying hues of blue and greenish-blue to bluish-green, and the colour of those obtained from Persia is permanent. Some years ago a variety was brought from Arabia, obtained from near Mount Sinai, in red sandstone ; and, although of a finer blue than the best Persian stones, it, unfortunately, did not keep its colour, often changing its hue most rapidly. Some specimens have retained their colour for a long time, but they can never become of value because of this liability to change. Major MacDonald exhibited at the London Exhibition of 1851 some very fine turquoises from this locality, but all suffered by exposure to light, and one that was purchased for a large sum of money had become by the end of a year almost worthless, having faded to a great extent.

Some fine specimens of turquoy have been obtained from Mexico, and the natives of that country were familiar with it, and used it in ancient times long before the discovery of their country by Europeans. It is obtained in New Mexico, and at Turquois Mount in Arizona. These gems are greenish in hue, and were highly valued for ornamental purposes by the original inhabitants. The mines were worked by the Spaniards 200 years ago, and many of the turquoises in the crown jewels of Spain were found there. The workings at that time were very prolific, but the water suddenly breaking in upon the Indians who were working in the mine, drowned about one hundred of them. The destruction was so great that the mine was abandoned, and remained closed until recently, when the industry was re-established after being neglected for over 200 years.

In Nevada, in the United States of America, fine blue specimens are found, approaching those found in Persia, but they are of small size. Thibet, China, Silesia, and Saxony are other localities where the turquois is found. At one time it was supposed to come from Russia also, but this appears to be erroneous, the idea most probably arising from the fact that a large number are cut and polished at Moscow, obtained at the fair of Nijni-Novgorod from Persian and Tartar merchants.

The turquois was largely used for amulets on account of its supposed possession of supernatural properties, and in the middle ages was used by the superstitious, as it was believed to give warning to its owner of an approaching calamity. This superstition has been alluded to by several English writers. It was also highly prized on account of many supposed virtues, but it was necessary that the gem should be received as a gift. This idea may be seen in the quotation of Shakespeare given above. Even to this day the Russians have a proverb,—" The turquois given by a loving hand carries with it happiness and good fortune."

It is doubtful whether the turquois was known to the ancients by its modern name, as it is not mentioned in their writings. That they were acquainted with the gem is certain, because several antique specimens are in the Vatican, and it is frequently discovered among the ruins of Egypt. It appears to have been first mentioned by an Arab of the twelfth century. The *Callais* of Pliny is generally regarded as the turquois, although the only information he gives about it is in the following sentence :—" Callais sapphirum imitatur, candidior et litoroso mari similis." Callais resembles the Lapis-lazuli (sapphirus), but of a lighter blue than the ocean). The *callaina* of that author is also referred to turquois, and, perhaps with good reason, he devotes quite a long chapter to it; he says that no stones were more easily imitated, which is true of the turquois.

An old description of the turquois is as follows :—" The turquois is a hard gem, yet full of beauty ; its colour is sky-blue out of a green, in which may be imagined a little milkish infusion. A clear sky, free from all clouds, will most excellently discover the beauty of a true turquois."

There is no doubt that it is a beautiful gem, and requires no foiling to set it off, a gold setting being all that is required to assist its appearance. It has the great advantage of not altering in colour by artificial light.

Those specimens which retain their colour without changing are said to belong to the "old rock," and are very scarce ; while those that lose their colour and become green are stated to be from the "new rock," although the distinction is evidently only discovered by experience. Ancient intaglios and cameos are in existence which have retained their colour unchanged until the present day. The Oriental lapidaries cut texts from the Koran on turquois, and filled these in with gold. There are also very good engravings on this gem extant. A necklace of twelve stones of a beautiful blue colour, but not of large size, was sold in the year 1808 for £360, each stone was engraved in relief with a figure of one of the twelve Cæsars. The Duke of Etruria possessed a turquois of the size of a hazel nut, having the image of Julius Cæsar engraved on it. A jeweller in Moscow at one time possessed a turquois two inches long, cut in the shape of a heart ; it was stated to have belonged originally to Shah Nadir, who wore it as an amulet. It was engraved with a verse of the Koran in the usual way. £780 was the price asked for it. A cameo in turquois engraved to represent the head of Tiberius, exists in Florence. There is also a fine cameo of this gem in the South Kensington Museum collection.

The Spaniards found that the turquois was considered by the Mexicans of more value than gold, and was largely used to ornament the temples of their gods ; an ear-ring of turquois being considered a fair exchange for a mule.

The market value of the turquois varies considerably. The Persian stones are always preferred for jewellery, and these when of large size and fine colour fetch extravagant prices, although, as previously stated, the best specimens are difficult to get out of Persia. The Persian ambassador to the Court of Louis XIV. presented to that monarch a large number of very fine specimens, which accounts for their presence in the French crown jewels.

The turquois is much used by Orientals to ornament their daggers, harness, swords, and pipes. At one time there was much demand for these gems, both in London and Paris, fine ring stones fetching as much as £10 to £40 each. A perfect stone of the size of a shilling, and of good depth, was stated to have been sold for £100, but there does not appear to be any fixed value for these gems.

The turquois is cut *en cabochon* on a leaden wheel and polished on a wooden one, and finished with rouge.

Odontolite or *Fossil Turquois* is a name given to the bone remains of extinct animals, these being coloured blue by phosphate of iron. They are brought from Siberia and have a striking resemblance, when cut, to the true turquois. They differ from it, however, by emitting an odour when gently heated, and besides the organic structure is easily detected by the aid of a microscope. When the true turquois is dissolved in hydrochloric acid, and ammonia added in excess, a blue coloured liquid results, showing the presence of copper. The bone turquois being coloured by iron does not give a blue colour when thus treated. Theophrastus mentions a fossil ivory having variegated colours of white and blue which was largely used by the jewellers of his time.

Turquois is rarely found in Australia; fairly good specimens have, however, been found at Hedi, King River, Victoria. The turquois from this locality exists with or without quartz in veins running through a slate rock. The colour of some portions is fairly good, but the veins are often very thin. I have not been able to ascertain whether stones cut from this turquois retain their colour, but a specimen from this locality which has been in the Museum collection for a few years appears to have perfectly retained its colour.

During the year 1894 a discovery of turquois was made on Mount Lorigan, in the Wagonga Division, Southern Mining District of New South Wales. At present little information is obtainable as to the value of the find.

TOURMALINE.

Cyrstalline system—Hexagonal, usually in striated prisms, with the crystals differently terminated at opposite ends.

Hardness—7—7·5.

Specific gravity—2·9—3·3.

Lustre—Vitreous.

Composition—Very variable and complex. All contain silicate of alumina, with boracic acid up to 10 per cent., iron, magnesia, lime, and soda, and from 1 to 2 per cent. of fluorine. Traces of phosphoric acid are usually found, and sometimes lithia.

As usually seen in New South Wales, the tourmaline is jet black and opaque, and is the variety *schorl*, a name thought to be derived from a village in Germany, and applied to this mineral by the miners of that locality. If all tourmalines were of this character, it would not be necessary to consider them here, because commercially this variety has no value.

When the tourmaline is red or pink, it is known as *Rubellite*, and when transparent is cut as a gem. The indigo-blue tourmaline is *Indicolite*. When of a Berlin-blue colour and transparent, it is cut as a gem, and is known commercially as *Brazilian Sapphire*. The red is *Brazilian Ruby*. The *Brazilian Emerald* is green and transparent, and of all the varieties is most largely used as a gem. The honey-yellow is called *Peridot of Ceylon*, and the colourless specimens are known as *Achroite*; so that the range of colour in the tourmaline is a wide one, and when we take into consideration that these differences of colour also denote differences of composition, we see how interesting these precious stones are from a scientific point of view.

The phenomena also exhibited by the tourmaline are remarkable, the most important being its power of polarizing light, and it has rendered the greatest assistance to physicists in their study of the properties and laws governing light. The discovery by Huyghens in the year 1678 of the polarization of light by double refraction, as exemplified by Iceland spar, paved the way for experiments with the tourmaline, when this property had been discovered in that gem. The discovery led to the use of the tourmaline in most subsequent experiments made with polarized light. The history of these investigations is most interesting and scientifically useful, but foreign to our present purpose.

Pyroelectricity, or that property certain substances have of acquiring electricity when heated, is best studied in the tourmaline; in fact it was first discovered in this mineral. Its power of attracting and then repelling hot ashes when placed among them, directed attention to this peculiarity of the tourmaline, and was on this account called by the Dutch the *ashes-drawer*. For further information concerning this phenomenon of pyroelectricity works on physics may be consulted, but the electrical properties of tourmaline when heated, may be determined by carefully heating the specimen in the flame of a candle, when minute pieces of paper, pith, or other light substances become attracted in a most marked manner.

It is generally supposed that the first tourmaline was brought from Ceylon, and the name is no doubt of Cingalese origin, but it appears to have been little thought of until the beginning of the eighteenth century, an account of it appearing in the Memoirs of the Academy of Sciences at Paris for the year 1717; so that in the list of precious stones the tourmaline may be considered to have been brought into use in comparatively recent times.

The powerful dichroism of this gem acts in a remarkable manner, and alone helps to identify it. Great care has to be taken in the cutting and polishing of these stones, to prevent this dichroism acting in an unsatisfactory manner. For instance, in cut and faceted specimens if the table is perpendicular to the principal axis of the crystal, most probably the gem will appear in its thicker portion opaque and black, but by making the table parallel with this axis the gem will present a brilliant and beautiful appearance; many of the green stones, or *Brazilian Emeralds*, vieing with the emerald for beauty of colour and appearance, having a fine play of colours, and often exhibiting two hues of green in the same stone. Even naturally the hues are not constant, and crystals have been found, one part of which are green, another part red. Some are crimson tipped with black, others yellowish mixed with carmine, and some are blue passing into green, while some very fine specimens found in America are red internally and green on the outside. In the Isle of Elba specimens are found which are red at one end, yellow in the middle, and black or brown at the other extremity.

The colourless tourmalines are very rare. They are found in Siberia and Elba, the best come from the latter locality, but are not usually sufficiently perfect or of sufficient size to be cut into gems.

Ceylon and India furnish a large quantity of these gem-stones, and a magnificent group of crystals, presented to Colonel Symes in 1799 by the King of Burmah, and now in the British Museum, has been valued at £1,000. It is the variety *rubellite*, or red tourmaline. That institution contains a splendid collection of tourmalines from nearly every locality where found—a specimen from the Tyrol showing both ends of the crystal having like faces is a very exceptional case, the tourmaline being remarkable for having the ends of the crystal differently formed, or showing in a marked manner the peculiarity known as *hemimorphism*. Siberia furnishes some fine specimens of various colours, ruby, purple, green, and other hues, but perhaps the most noted locality is at Mount Mica, a spur of streaked mountain near Paris, Maine, United States of America. From an area of about 30 square feet, nearly forty varieties have been obtained, some being very rare and beautiful. These gems were discovered by two mineralogical students when searching for specimens (an illustration of the advantages of a scientific education), a few broken fragments of crystals leading to an examination of the locality, which resulted in the discovery of a granite ledge, perforated with cavities filled with tourmalines and other minerals. An enormous quantity of gems has been taken from this locality since the discovery, and specimens are to be found in all the principal European collections. Good specimens have also been found in many other parts of America, but, perhaps, the most famous locality is Brazil. Fine specimens are found there, and it has been the principal market for which the European jewellers have obtained their supplies for very many years. The tourmaline commonly occurs in granite, gneiss, mica-slate, chlorite-slate, and granular limestone, and is usually found in alluvial deposits with tin. It is not an uncommon mineral, although, unfortunately, the majority of the specimens are black.

The tourmaline is cut upon a leaden or zinc wheel with emery, and polished with tripoli powder. The value depends upon the colour, quality, and size of the specimens, that of one of exceptional colour and purity, and of five carats weight, is given by Mr. Streeter at £20.

As it is not certain that the tourmaline was known to the ancients, there is a fine field for inquiry whether this gem was described by ancient writers under another name, but the probability is that its electrical properties were known to them. We may assume, however, that it was not used at that time as a gem, although seals were made of it.

Theophrastus tells us of the *lyncurium*, that it was a very hard stone which could with difficulty be cut, that seals were formed of it, that it was transparent, of a fiery colour, almost like that of yellow amber, that it attracted light bodies, such as chaff, shavings of wood, leaves, feathers, and bits of thin iron and copper leaf in the same manner as amber; that the ancients procured it from Ethiopia. Theophrastus does not state whether the *lyncurium* only attracted when heated, and there arises the difficulty which has not yet been settled. At present no tourmaline is known to attract until it is heated.

In the catalogue of the collection of natural curiosities belonging to Paul Hermann, which sale took place in June, 1711, at Leyden, we find listed *Chrysolithus Turmale Zeylon*. This, without doubt, is our tourmaline. Originally the stone was considered as a chrysolite, and perhaps it may have been mentioned under that name in accounts of Ceylon prior to this date.

It is very probable that the tourmaline will some day be in greater request for ornamental purposes than it is at present. Human nature is always seeking after the wonderful and the mysterious. The same sentiment which prevails in reference to such gem-stones as *Flèches d'Amour* or *Love's Arrows*, which are hair-like crystals of rutile or other mineral, enclosed in quartz, will some day perhaps be extended to the tourmaline. It is not to be expected that the value will greatly increase, but anyone finding tourmalines of colour and quality equal to those of Brazil or North America may be sure of good returns.

The characteristic form of the crystals, often almost triangular, is sufficient in many instances to determine this gem, and this, together with differences in hardness and specific gravity, separate this stone from those gems which it somewhat resembles; the presence of fluorine is often very market.

The tourmaline occurs in large prisms in the New England district, and is common in the granite there; it also occurs in many other localities throughout the Colony, large crystals being found in the Uralla district, while masses, weighing 20lb., have been seen.

QUARTZ AND ITS VARIETIES.

Crystalline system—Hexagonal when crystallized.
Hardness—7.
Specific gravity—2·5—2·8.
Lustre—Vitreous.
Composition—Silica, SiO_2.   Silicon or Silicium $= 46·67$, oxygen $= 53·33$ per cent.

The most transparent and vitreous varieties of the quartz family are known as rock crystal, and have been used very largely for many purposes in all ages. Rock crystal was considered of great importance for ornamental purposes during the cinque-cento period. At the present time its greatest value is for optical purposes, administering to the comfort of a large number of the human race. It is also largely used in the cheaper kinds of jewellery, and is known by the various names of Bristol, Welsh, Irish, Cornish, and Californian diamonds. It is also known and employed in jewellery under the name of "white stone."

Its original name of crystal was given to it because of its supposed origin from ice. Claudianus, one of the writers of antiquity, calls it "ice hardened into stone." Orpheus calls it "the translucent image of the Eternal Light," and suggests its use as a burning glass to light the sacrificial flame. The natives of India believed it to the mother or husk of the diamond, and called the diamond the ripe and the crystal the unripe diamond.

Sir Thomas Browne, in his work on *Vulgar Errors*, 1646, says that the opinion was then prevalent that the crystal was congealed ice. The word crystal, by being derived from the Greek *Krustallos*, meaning ice, stamps the fact indelibly upon the history of this stone.

The Romans were particularly partial to rock crystal, and employed it largely for articles of household use, as well as for personal adornment. They paid large sums for vessels made of it, and the art of forming these from such a material reached at that time a very high state of perfection. Of the patient labour necessary to the delicate task of hollowing out vessels of such a character, it is difficult to form an estimate.

The various museums of Europe contain valuable collections of crystal cups, vases, goblets, &c., showing that at one time these articles were brought into extensive use. A crystal ewer in the South Kensington Museum, and for which £450 was paid, is 8½ inches high, and has a diameter of 5½ inches. It belongs to the 9th or 10th century, and is carved in low relief, with birds, animals, and foliage. By an inventory made in Paris in 1791, the crown jewels of France contained crystal goblets, vases, &c., some of which were beautifully engraved, and were altogether valued at one million francs. One urn, measuring 9½ inches in diameter, and 9 inches high, was engraved with the figure of Noah asleep, his children holding a covering. This urn cost £4,000.

Perhaps the superstition that crystal cups were incapable of holding poison, betraying its presence by becoming obscured, or breaking, had something to do with the demand for articles of this description during mediæval times.

The Emperor Nero is said to have possessed some magnificent cups of crystal, engraved with subjects from the Iliad, and he is charged with breaking two of these in a fit of anger on hearing of the loss of his kingdom ; one of these cost him a sum equal to £600 of our money, a very large amount in those days.

In India the natives hollow rock crystal into cups and vases of surprising thinness. The Chinese also make articles from it, to which they attach great value, but their work is inferior to that of the Indian workmen.

Rock crystal is very lustrous when perfectly clear, and is often found beautifully crystallized, the hexagonal prisms often being terminated at both ends by hexagonal pyramids. Fine specimens are found at Lake George, in Herkimer County, and at other counties in the adjacent regions in New York State, America. They are known and sold as " Lake George diamonds," and are found in calcareous sandstone.

The crystal employed for optical purposes comes principally from Brazil, although not superior to that obtained elsewhere. It is much cheaper, however.

Rock crystal is sometimes obtained of immense size ; some remarkable specimens from Brazil and Japan were exhibited at Philadelphia in 1876. A group of crystals in the museum of the University of Naples weighs nearly half a ton. A crystal belonging to a gentleman at Milan measures 3¼ feet in length, its weight being about 870 lb. Another in Paris is 3 feet in diameter, and weighs 8 cwt. About a century since a drusy cavity was opened at Zinken, affording 1,000 cwt. of rock crystal, and at that time brought about £60,000. One crystal weighed 800 lb.

Madagascar has produced large blocks of rock crystal, and the sand of this island contains innumerable crystals. Switzerland produces fine specimens ; near St. Gothard is a noted locality, while the neighbourhood of Mont Blanc yields fine clear crystals, and the collection of these gives employment to many of the inhabitants of Chamouni. In 1867, at the Galgenstock, above the Tiefen Glacier, a discovery was made by a party of tourists of a magnificent collection of crystallized quartz, a cave in the granite yielding more than a thousand crystals, all of large size, weighing from 50 lb. each to upwards of 3 cwt. They were, however, of dark colour. One crystal, known as the " Grandfather," weighs 276 lb., while another, the "King," weighs 255 lb.

In the cavities of the snow white marble of Carrara, in Tuscany, crystals are found of great beauty. Small doubly terminated crystals are also found in the limestone of the Levis and Hudson River formations, in America, and are locally known as "Quebec diamonds." At Crystal Mountain, Arkansas, U.S.A., and in the regions around Hot Springs for about 40 miles, large quantities are found. In a cavity 30 feet long and 6 feet high, several tons of crystals were found, the sides being entirely covered with them. Waggon loads of these crystals are taken to Hot Springs by the farmers in the neighbourhood, who obtain them when work on the farm is slack. They are sold to the local dealers, to be disposed of principally as mementos. A specimen from this locality in the museum collection is composed of beautiful crystals, showing doubly terminated prisms. The manufacturer of artificial gems has not even passed these crystals by, many of the specimens sold as " Lake George diamonds " being made of " paste," a glass containing a large percentage of lead. Although having the lustre of the real stones, their deficiency in hardness, and increased specific gravity, at once determine them. They are also fusible in the blowpipe flame, while quartz is infusible. Rock crystal has been employed very successfully in the imitation of the ruby, sapphire, and other gems, by artificial colouring,—first the stone is heated, and then plunged into prepared solutions to give it the required colour.

The cavities frequently found in quartz crystals have given rise to much speculation and investigation, many of these cavities containing liquid (these are Pliny's Enhydros or Enhygros). While at one time these investigations were thought to lead to definite conclusions, as to the origin of these *lacunæ*, the results have not confirmed these hopes. The contained liquid has been found to vary much ; in some it is only water, sometimes water holding carbonic acid in solution, sometimes liquid carbonic acid, while supersaturated solutions of chloride of sodium have been found, minute crystals of rock salt being visible within these cavities under the microscope, with fairly high objectives. These cavities at times are full, others contain a bubble which moves about on turning the crystal. But while so important from a scientific point of view, they do not compare for ornamental purposes with those specimens enclosing mineral crystals, such as fine fibres or slender crystals of rutile, or other substances ; these are known by many fantastic names, as *Love's Arrows*, *Cupid's Nets*, *Venus's Hair*, &c. ; they are often cut for brooches.

In America a good trade was at one time carried on in these gem minerals. They are there cut into oval seals and charms, for use in jewellery. These enclosed minerals are very plentiful in American crystals, while in Japan and Madagascar large masses are found. They are not uncommon, and are found in many parts of the world, including this Colony. In the New England district crystals are often found enclosing cassiterite, while in California they have been found enclosing stibnite, hæmatite, dolomite, chlorite, and many other minerals, while hornblende is of common occurrence.

When those specimens containing bubbles in the liquid of the cavities of sufficient sizes to be readily seen, they are cut for gems, and sell readily up to £5 each. They are often met with in jewels of the Cinque-cento period.

The value of ordinary rock crystal in the rough varies much, according to quality, but pieces of large size bring high prices. It is cut on a copper wheel with emery, and polished with tripoli.

Natural crystals are often so small that an ounce weight will contain between 7,000 and 8,000 stones, all of which are perfect, and doubly terminated. In this colony these small crystals are often mistaken for diamonds, but when seen under a lens they are found to be hexagonal, while the diamond belongs to the cubical system.

When rock crystal varies in colour it has characteristic names, the yellow is known as *citrine*, or *false topaz*, the brown as *Cairngorm*, or *smoky quartz*, and the black as *Morion*.

The remaining members of the quartz family will now be considered. The principal of these are agate, amethyst, avanturine, cat's-eye, chalcedony, chrysoprase, carnelian, jasper, heliotrope, milky quartz, onyx, plasma, prase, rose quartz, sard, sardonyx, besides many varieties of these. A collector may spend much time in making a collection of pretty pebbles, but the one word *quartz*, with its distinctive names, will probably embrace the whole of them.

In this colony large crystals are found in many localities, some obtained at the tin mines of New England weighing nearly 1 cwt. It would be tedious to enumerate the many localities whence rock crystal has been obtained. Mineral enclosures have also been found at various localities.

Amethyst.

Of all the quartz varieties the amethyst has (next to rock crystal) been the most highly valued, and the most frequently used for ornamental purposes through all ages. It is perhaps to-day one of the most popular of this class of gem stones, and although much cheapened of late years, continues to be largely cut and used for rings, brooches, pendants, pins, &c.

It is necessary to bear in mind that the *Oriental amethyst* is allied to the sapphire, is a rare and valuable gem, and is certainly not to be purchased for a small sum, although vendors of ornamental stones often attach the name of Oriental to the quartz variety. It may safely be considered that nearly the whole of the amethyst sold in jewellers' shops belongs to the quartz family.

All those specimens of quartz having a purplish or violet hue, and transparent, come under the name of amethyst. The colour is supposed to be due to a trace of manganese, but Heintz, who analysed a Brazilian specimen, considered the colour to be owing to a compound of iron and soda. The deepest shades are, when cut, less brilliant than the lighter, and it is supposed that this accounts for the fact that the ancient lapidaries preferred to exercise their art upon the lighter coloured stones.

A dark-coloured amethyst does not, as a rule, belong to ancient times; although C. W. King, M.A., says he has seen perhaps the grandest Greek portrait in existence, a head of Mithridates (probably) cut in a large amethyst of the deepest violet colour, and which was found a century ago in India.

In early times the amethyst seems to have been a favourite stone for cameos and engravings. Many Egyptian and Etruscan scarabei were amethyst. A very fine gem of this variety of quartz fell into the hands of Napoleon during his invasion of Prussia; or, as Mr. Streeter puts it, "of which the Prussian treasury was robbed during the Napoleonic wars." It was engraved with a likeness of the Emperor Trajan. Another historical gem of this class is a bust of Antonia, the daughter of Mark Antony. An engraving by Dioscorides is in the National Library of Paris.

The name is from the Greek *a* not, *methuo* to be drunk; the amethyst being regarded by the ancients as a preservative against drunkenness. It was thus considered the most suitable for drinking cups, on account of its being a protection against intoxication. Pliny says that the gem was so called, from the fact of its approaching near to the colour of wine.

In the middle ages it was believed to dispel sleep, sharpen the intellect, and to be an antidote against poison. It was in such repute, that in the middle of the seventeenth century a specimen of amethyst was considered to be worth as much as a diamond of equal weight; but since that time, perhaps owing to its being found in large quantities in Brazil, America, and elsewhere, the value has much depreciated. Queen Charlotte had an amethyst necklace made of well matched and very perfect stones, and it was valued at one time at £2,000, but Mr. Streeter considers it doubtful if it would now realise £100.

The amethyst is cut in various ways, but the best form is that of the brilliant, the table or flat part of the stone being slightly domed instead of quite flat. The majority of these stones are cut in Germany, the labour in England being too expensive. A copper wheel with emery is used in the cutting, and the polishing is done on tin with tripoli. It takes a very fine polish.

The greatest fault the amethyst has is that in artificial light it loses a part of its beauty, appearing of a blackish hue. It harmonises perfectly with gold and pearls, and no doubt will continue to increase in popularity now that the taste for this gem has revived.

The amethyst is found in numerous localities in the United States of America, and in Mexico; those from Guanajuata, which have a world-wide reputation, are found in large quantities, and range in colour from the most delicate pink to the deepest red. The crystals are frequently light in colour at the base, but much darker at the termination. The colour of the amethyst can be removed by heating, and this treatment is carefully used to remove spots and faulty colouring in a gem, as the stone is thus made of a uniform colour. This is a very common mode of treatment to add to the colour of some gems, notably the topaz and the Oriental carnelian. One method of "burning" precious stones is to roll them up in a piece of sponge and burn them with it, or, as is done with the amethyst, to place the stones in a crucible with unslacked lime or iron filings, and heat them until they are quite clear. The process requires the greatest care, or the gem may be hopelessly destroyed.

Besides the localities already mentioned, the amethyst is found in Spain, India, Persia, Siberia, Hungary, Saxony, and Ceylon, in beautiful crystals. Near Oberstein, in Germany, it is found in a trap rock, in geodes in agate; these geodes being sometimes as much as 2 feet in diameter, hollow, and filled with crystallized amethyst of a fine colour. Similar geodes are found in other parts of the world. The amethyst is found in many localities in New South Wales, but of little value for cutting purposes. It is found in geodes in the basalt at Kiama, also at Eden, Boggabri, Brewongle, Emmaville, and many other places.

Agate.

This is virtually a variegated chalcedony, composed of differently coloured bands, sometimes with characteristic markings due to visible impurities. Agate forming varieties of quartz consists, besides chalcedony, of carnelian, jasper, quartz, and sometimes amethyst. Two or more of these combined, and presenting a diversity of spots or bands, form the agate; and according to the distribution of these bands or dendritic markings, so the stone is known by characteristic names; it is called *banded agate* when the bands are delicate parallel lines of white, pale or dark brown, or blackish colours, sometimes a portion shows bluish and other shades. The lines are generally wavy or circular. These bands are the edges of layers of deposition, the agate having been formed by a deposit of silica from solution intermittently supplied, in irregular cavities in rocks, and deriving their concentric waving from the irregularities of the walls of the cavity; this variety is also known as *ribbon agate*, and when the colours are very sharply defined and a portion blackish, it is known as *onyx agate*. When the variously coloured bands are in angular patterns it is known as *fortification agate*, from a supposed resemblance to the outlines of a fortification. Then we have other specimens known as *jasper agate*, and when resembling a breccia, as *brecciated agate* and others with fanciful names as *zone agate, clouded agate*, and *wood agate*. When the visible markings somewhat resemble moss enclosed, the specimen is known as *moss agate* or *Mocha stone*. This variety came originally from Arabia, but large quantities have been found in America.

The beauty of the agate depends principally on the colour, brilliancy, and character of the material forming the larger portion of the stone. Besides being manufactured into articles for ornamental purposes, the agate is a most useful stone in many other ways. It is made into burnishers for the gilder, mortars are made of it for the pulverisation of hard minerals in analysis, and the working parts of delicate balances are also made of it. In olden times it used to be largely used for the manufacture of cups and vases. A very fine specimen was the two-handled cup engraved with bacchanalian subjects, and presented by Charles III of France in the ninth century to the Abbey of St. Denys; it was used to hold the wine at the coronation of the French kings. The Greeks and Romans prized the agate, and it was with them a favourite stone for engraving. One of the largest and best specimens was a portrait of Alexander the Great.

It has been stated that at the sack of Delhi, the British soldiers destroyed a large number of magnificent agate cups, an act which, if true, is worthy of the greatest condemnation.

The distribution of the impurities in agate often takes fantastic forms (sometimes called nature-pictures), a specimen in the British Museum showing what, with a little stretch of imagination, may be construed into the portrait of the poet Chaucer. A specimen in the Florence Gallery has a Cupid running, and one in the Strawberry Hills collection has a woman in profile, and another which is considered to resemble Voltaire. Pliny states that King Pyrrhus possessed a natural agate, in which was depicted Apollo playing on the lyre and the nine Muses with their attributes.

Nearly the whole of the cut and polished agates come from Oberstein and Idar, in the Duchy of Oldenburg, Germany, where the manufacture of such articles has been carried on for more than 300 years. The supplies of later years have been obtained principally from Uruguay and Brazil. A quantity of the raw material from these localities, ranging from 10 to 100 tons, is often sold by auction in lots to suit purchasers, the average price obtained being about 1s. per lb. Many hundreds of the inhabitants of these towns are constantly employed in the cutting and polishing of these stones, although the trade is not nearly so flourishing as in former times, cheap silver jewellery having to a great extent superseded them.

The mills used in the cutting are generally driven by water power. The grinding wheels are of large size—some 5 or 7 feet in diameter. The workmen lie face downwards on a bench made for the purpose, and hold the stone against the wheels, their feet resting against supports. This method of working gives them great purchase, and the work is done in a much shorter time than is the usual way of grinding. This, together with the cheap labour, enables these polished stones to be sold cheaply.

Agates readily lend themselves to artificial staining, some portions being more porous than others. There are many processes whereby the desired result is obtained.

Wood Agate

is found in great abundance in Colorado, California, and other Western States of America; and among the many wonderful sights of this prolific country is the solidified forest known as Chalcedony Park, situated 8 miles south of Corrizo, in Apache County, Arizona. Here enormous trees, that were originally more than 150 feet in height, have been transformed into agate and jasper. Over a large area these trees lie scattered in all directions, and present a phenomenon perhaps unparalleled. Dr. P. H. Dudley has examined these trees microscopically, and has found that some of them belonged to the well-known Australian genus *Araucaria*.

The preparing of these agatised trees for the market has been taken in hand by a company. One section sent to New York in 1888 measured 40½ inches by 34 inches on the top; it was 36 inches high, and weighed 2¼ tons. It took four months to grind down and polish the top. This is perhaps the finest piece of hard stone polishing of this character ever undertaken.

The best specimens of agate come from India, Brazil, and Uruguay. In the rivers of the latter country agate nodules of considerable size are found, and they are there in large quantity. The beach pebbles found in the South of England were exported in large quantities to Germany to be cut; also those known as Scotch pebbles, and sold in Edinburgh as such, are generally cut in Oberstein.

In this Colony agate is plentiful in many localities, although at present it cannot compare with the Indian or Brazilian specimens. It is common in basalt at Kiama, in diorite at Mittagong, and is found in beds of many rivers and old drifts of New South Wales.

Chalcedony.

May be regarded as a mixture of crystalline and amorphous silica, or true quartz with hydrous silica or opal. It is usually found filling cavities in amygdaloidal rocks, and has generally a mammillated (with large spheroidal surfaces), or botryoidal (with smaller spheroidal surfaces) appearance; it is usually of a semi-opaque, milky-white colour, and has a waxy or greasy lustre. Pure chalcedony has little value for ornamental purposes, only the coloured varieties (and these have characteristic names) being used. It was named chalcedony from the first being obtained at Chalcedon, in Asia Minor. It is never found crystallized. A white chalcedony with minute red spots, like blood, has received the name of "St. Stephen's Stone."

Perhaps the best known member of the chalcedonic group of the quartz family is the *carnelian*. This is mostly a pale red stone, characterised by its translucency or semi-opacity; it is most probable that the name was given to it on account of its colour, which can be intensified by heat. Some specimens are almost blood-red in colour, while inferior ones are wax-yellow to brown. The blood-red variety is considered the most valuable for ornamental purposes, the pale red coming next. It receives a fine polish, and these stones were at one time largely cut for seals, and in ancient times for cameos, to which purpose many specimens lend themselves in a marked degree. The Greeks and Romans used it largely for this purpose. The oldest Greek specimens of engraved carnelians known are in the collection of the Emperor of Germany, one representing a winged Jupiter, while another is engraved with a draped figure of Venus. In several of the European collections good specimens of these engraved stones are seen.

A large trade has been carried on with carnelians in India for more than 2000 years, but the value of these stones has much decreased during late years. The carnelian is found in large quantities in Brazil, India, and other places, and this fact, together with the artificial staining of inferior specimens, as carried on at Oberstein and Idar, have been instrumental in bringing their value down to almost the bare cost of cutting. The carnelian is cut on a leaden wheel with emery, and polished on a wooden one with pumice stone.

Jewellers and lapidaries distinguish the carnelian by the following names :—

1. Masculine, the dark red variety.
2. Feminine, the pale red stones.
3. Sard, the brown passing into yellow.
4. Sardonyx, when layers of the sard alternate with layers of white chalcedony.
5. Carnelian onyx, when the blood-red stripes pass into white.
6. Carnelian beryl, a whitish yellow variety.

The carnelian is found in nodular masses, and often as rolled pebbles ; at Baroach, in India, pebbles of great beauty are found, also in the rivers of Uruguay. It is largely cut and used for rings, seals, watch pendants, beads, and other ornaments. By artificial treatment its beauty can be greatly enhanced. As noted above, the sard is only a yellowish brown carnelian. Specimens from India are of great beauty, while those obtained from the neighbourhood of Babylon were by the nations of antiquity esteemed as of great value. The different varieties of chalcedony are common in this Colony, although rarely of good colour.

Chrysoprase

is an apple green chalcedony, its green colour owing to oxide of nickel. Although mentioned in the writings of antiquity, it is doubtful whether the stones were identical with those of modern times, because no works of ancient times have come down to us in true chrysoprase. It is found in Silesia embedded in serpentine, and was at one time in great request in Prussia, the kings only allowing the mines to be opened once in three years, and they then kept the finest specimens for themselves. Frederick the Great used the chrysoprase in adorning the Palace of Sans Souci. It was also used for the interior decoration of the walls of St. Wenzel's Chapel, in the Cathedral of Prague, which was built in the fourteenth century. In the Royal Palace of Potsdam there are two tables formed from chrysoprase, which are 3 feet long, 2 feet broad, and 2 inches thick. A very fine intaglio of light green chrysoprase, and of oval shape, representing the head of Ariadne, is in the Hope collection.

The chrysoprase takes a high polish, is really a very pretty stone, and has the advantage of being found in large pieces. During the last year or two, attempts have been made to revive the taste for this stone for ornamental purposes, but they have only partly succeeded. Klaproth the chemist, was the first to discover the presence of nickel in chrysoprase, and also the fact that the stone contained a small quantity of water. If by the influence of heat the water is removed, the beauty of the stone is destroyed ; for this reason it is supposed that the nickel is present in the form of a hydrate. The working of the stone has to be done with great care, on account of the ease with which the colour is partly destroyed; it is principally cut *en cabochon*, with small facets round the edge of the upper side. The greater number of cut stones of chrysoprase are done at Warmbrunn, in Silesia. At Oberstein a green colour is artificially given to chalcedony by means of the salts of nickel, or of chromic acid, it then having the appearance of chrysoprase. The value depends on the colour and its freedom from flaws. Besides the locality mentioned the chrysoprase is found in America, principally in a vein of serpentine, in the nickel mines at Nickel Mount, near the town of Riddles, Douglas County, Oregon; it is found here in veins over an inch in thickness, and stones several inches square could be made from it. The colour is good. The name signifies " golden leek," and is in reference to its colour.

Stones much resembling the chrysoprase are *prase* and *plasma*, the former being translucent in appearance, and of a muddy olive-green colour. The name is from *prason*, signifying a " leek," and was also given on account of its colour. *Plasma* is a translucent variety of chalcedonic quartz, of a brighter green than prase. The name signifies " image," or anything formed or imitated. It is found in ancient ruins, and was no doubt confounded with the chrysoprase. It is often speckled with white.

Heliotrope or Bloodstone.

Another green stone is the *heliotrope* or *bloodstone*, and is identified by the presence of minute bright red spots disseminated throughout the green jasperoid base; hence its name of bloodstone. There is in the Royal collection in Paris a bust of Jesus Christ executed in this material, the red spots being so arranged that they stand out like real drops of blood. There is a tradition, believed in the age of superstition, that at the crucifixion the blood of Christ, falling upon a dark green jasper, produced the red spots.

The stone was used as a talisman by the Egyptians, and was in great request during the Byzantine and Renaissance periods. Egyptian and Babylonian intagli have been found cut in this stone, but engravings are rare. The name heliotrope is from the Greek, and was so named because of the idea that when immersed in water it changed the image of the sun into blood-red. Pliny states that the sun could be viewed in it as in a mirror, and that it made visible its eclipses. Marbodus, in the eleventh century, in his poem on gems, also speaks of it as having this property. It is found in large quantities in India, Bokhara, Siberia, Tartary, and in many other places. It is a favourite stone with engravers, and crests and monograms are engraved upon it. It is largely used for signet rings. Cups and other ornamental objects of art are also made of it. It is much used for pendants and small articles of this character.

Jasper.

This is the opaque variety of quartz, presenting a compact texture, and destitute of any crystalline structure. In colour it ranges from green through the reds and browns, and from yellow to grey and bluish. It takes a fine polish. It was a favourite material for engravings in ancient times. The breastplate made for the high priest of the Israelites contained an engraved jasper. Fine portraits of the Roman Emperors were cut in this stone, including that of Nero. The head of Minerva, in jasper, belonging to the Vatican collection, is considered to be the finest intaglio in existence. The Imperial seal of China is made of jasper, and in almost all countries articles are manufactured in this stone for use or adornment. Jasper should be opaque on the edges of thin splinters, and be infusible before the blow-pipe flame. The Egyptian jasper, characterised by intense red or ochre-yellow tints passing into chesnut brown, and sometimes spotted with black, was found near Cairo, and extensively used in ancient times. Yellow jasper is found near the Bay of Smyrna, in Greece, and is used in the Florentine mosaic work under the name of *pietra dura*. The red jasper, so largely used by the Roman engravers, came from Argos, in Greece. Five hundred years before the Christian era a writer speaks of the " grass-green jasper which rejoices the eye of man and is looked on with pleasure by the immortals." The emeralds spoken of by the Roman and Greek authors are considered to be green jasper, because pillars of their temples were cut out of one piece—a work not likely with the emerald. An old writer states that if a jasper be hung about the neck it will strengthen the stomach.

A large quantity of jasper is cut and polished for articles of adornment, the value in Europe in the rough ranging from 1s. up to 50s. a pound, the price depending upon the evenness of texture and the colour. A variety, beautifully banded with different shades of brown, is known as *ribbon jasper;* the original came from Egypt. If agate and jasper are combined in the same specimens, they are agate-jasper or jasper-agate, according to the predominance of the one or the other. The "Pebbles of Rennes," mentioned by Haüy, are composed of agate and jasper of a very deep red, interspersed with small round or oval spots of reddish or yellowish white, and were used for ornamental boxes and other similar work.

There is no doubt about the regard with which the jasper was held, and being of common occurrence it could be easily obtained. In the Scriptures the jasper is often spoken of, and its glory is chosen to represent the New Jerusalem. The quietness and rich solidity of articles manufactured in the best kinds of jasper appeal to the better taste of those who admire ornaments because they are good rather than pretty.

Jasper occurs in large quantities in the Ural Mountains, also in the Altai Mountains, in Russia. The jasper from the latter locality is very fine; it is worked up by the local polishing works into large objects, vases, &c. A large oval bowl, 20 feet across, was made here. It is preserved in the Imperial Hermitage. Works of art from this material embellish many of the Imperial palaces. At the present time no less than eight quarries are being worked in the Altai Mountains, from which a large quantity of porphyry, blue and green jasper, and other rocks of this character are obtained.

In this Colony the carnelian is fairly common. Good coloured stones occur in the basaltic country about the Tweed River. The chrysoprase does not appear to have been yet found. Jasper is very abundant, being distributed over many portions of New South Wales.

Onyx.

This stone differs from the agate by having its different bands arranged in parallel layers. Light and dark chalcedonic quartz arranged alternately, form the onyx, the most frequent colours being black, or very dark brown, and white. The name is stated to be derived from a supposed resemblance to the finger-nail. The finest specimens are brought from India, in pieces having a circular form, and having a white stripe running round the centre. The more of these concentric rings or layers, the more valuable the stone. The onyx was at one time in much request for cameos and for carvings in relief on costly vessels, the figure being cut out of the light layer and standing in relief upon the dark ground.

A very fine specimen of this character, and one having great historical interest, is that in the possession of the Canton of Schaffhausen. It is engraved with the figure of a female wearing a crown of honour, and holding in one hand a horn of plenty, in the other a Mercury's staff. It was engraved about the year A.D. 70, and was supposed to have been brought from Constantinople. How it came into the possession of the Swiss is not known for certain, but is supposed to have been part of the "spoils of war" from the victory of Granson.

A very fine specimen is the Mantuan vase, the figures representing Ceres and Triptolemus in search of Proserpine. The vase is 7 inches high and 2½ inches broad, and is cut from a single stone. It is supposed to belong to the middle of the second century.

Several very fine specimens of these works of art are also to be found in the different European museums and art collections, although it is to be supposed that some of these specimens of works of art are agate, as authorities differ.

The onyx is sometimes found in masses of large size, and in the Church of St. Peter, at Rome, are to be seen six small pillars, each made from single specimens.

E

Pliny wrote much about the onyx. He mentioned thirty columns of large size in the banquet-hall of Callistus, and this variety of quartz is often mentioned in the writings of ancient authors, as well as in the Bible. In olden times, true to the mysterious properties ascribed to rare and precious things, the onyx was supposed to cause strife and melancholy, and also to be a cure for epileptic fits. Mithridates is stated to have had made 2,000 cups of the onyx; certainly a royal encouragement of the arts and sciences. In the ancient tombs and temples of Cyprus were found, it is stated, numerous engraved onyxes, supposed to have been worn not less than three or four centuries before the Christian era.

The rosaries worn by the fakirs of India, from the time of Pliny until the present, were mostly onyx beads, and these are sometimes sold at a high figure. Unfortunately, since the introduction of artificial staining, the onyx has been manufactured wholesale, and its value has correspondingly decreased. It is well that so many of the ancient carved onyxes have been preserved, because, beyond their historic value, the workmanship is exquisite. The time necessary to be taken, and the patient labour required to be expended upon these works of art, are hardly possible in this hurrying age, although some very fair work has been done in modern times.

Besides India, good onyx is found in Arabia, Russia, Germany, South America, &c.; but the Mexican onyx, so called, is aragonite, containing small quantities of the oxides of iron and manganese. To the presence of these is due the coloured bands which make this rock so much admired. It was used in large quantities by the ancient Mexicans, its softness enabling it to be readily carved. Aragonite is carbonate of lime, but differs from calcite in that it crystallizes in the rhombic system, while calcite is hexagonal. This is a well-marked case of dimorphism. Mexican onyx is a beautiful material fit for decorative purposes of the highest class, as can be seen from the specimens in the Museum collection, but too soft for gems.

When the white zone of the onyx is so thin that it appears semi-transparent, the stone is known as *nicolo*, a corruption of the Italian word meaning "little onyx."

The onyx is much prized in some countries at the present time, and is much used for fine art jewellery, associated with diamonds and pearls, although the imitation onyx has reached that perfection that it is difficult to detect it from the real. The prices obtained for carefully-selected stones may be considered satisfactory, although the value does not appear to be a fixed one. The onyx is stated to occur in this colony in the neighbourhood of Narrabri.

Cat's-eye

is a yellowish-green or yellowish-brown variety of chalcedonic quartz, semi-transparent, and when cut *en cabochon* presents a silky lustre, resulting from the admixture of asbestos, thus giving to the stone a fibrous appearance. The stones are cut so that they are brought slightly to a ridge, this having the advantage of showing more perfectly the chatoyant nature of this stone, the top of the ridge showing as a line.

The quartz variety of the cat's-eye is not to be compared with the true or chrysoberyl cat's-eye, in comparison with which it is almost valueless; besides, the true cat's-eye is much harder, and has a higher specific gravity. When held so that the light strikes the stone obliquely, the appearance somewhat resembles the contracted pupil of the eye of the cat, hence the name.

A greenish variety is found massive and in large quantities near Hof, in Bavaria, and has been largely cut during late years into ornamental stones, gems of this character having come into request in several countries, especially America. Small rounded pebbles of good quality are found in Ceylon, some of which exhibit the cat's-eye peculiarity in very great perfection. Large quantities of these are cut into gem-stones by the Cingalese. The peculiar silky appearance of this stone cannot be mistaken when once seen. It is only necessary to remember the resemblance between the true cat's-eye and the quartz variety, and the determination of the latter is not difficult. Ancient writers called this stone wolf's-eye, and also *oculus belus*, as it was dedicated to the Assyrian god Belus. A very fine specimen is in the South Kensington Museum. The quartz cat's-eye has been obtained in the Western district of New South Wales, but the exact locality is not stated.

Avanturine.

Another variety of the quartz family having somewhat the character of the cat's-eye is the avanturine; this is a translucent stone, generally of a brownish-red colour, more rarely greenish. It has disseminated throughout the material minute particles of mica, and when this stone is cut and polished with a rounded surface, the glittering particles give to the stone a very fine appearance. It is found principally in Siberia, and does not appear to be of common occurrence. It is only used to a limited extent as an ornamental stone, although often used to decorate small articles. Fine specimens have been found at Cape de Gata in Spain, also in India. The green variety appears to have a small quantity of copper in its composition. A peculiar kind of mica schist, of a reddish colour, occurring in many localities is used for ornamental purposes, and is frequently sold for avanturine.

Imitation avanturine, often seen in articles manufactured in Italy, is a reddish-brown spangled glass, and was originally made at Murano, near Venice. Of course, it is less hard than the natural stones, and less durable, but is often far more beautiful in appearance. The origin of the term is supposed to have arisen from the fact that a glass-maker accidentally let fall some brass filings into the glass pot, and was surprised to find that the product presented a beautifully spangled appearance. As this was formed by accident, the word avanturine was used to denote its formation. As the term is one purely of a physical character, it is not restricted to one stone. Besides the quartz variety, we have *avanturine feldspar*, or "sunstone," so that the term is used in its broadest sense.

Besides these various varieties of quartz we have several other distinct varieties that are but little used for ornamental purposes. One is *rose quartz*, a delicate pink stone, having all the characters of massive quartz. Then there is *milky quartz*, which is opalescent or milky, and the various forms of smoky quartz. These are of little value.

It may appear remarkable that quartz is found under so many different forms and conditions, but when we consider that the element *silicon* is to the inorganic world what carbon is to the organic portion, forming the basis of the majority of the combinations of its rocks and many of its minerals, as carbon forms the basis of its vegetation, it ceases to be a surprise to us. In the early stages of the earth, silica played a most important part, long before the crust had sufficiently cooled to allow those elements that only act in the cold, as it were, to take their proper place. Silica forms a very large portion of the rocky crust of the earth, perhaps one-fifth.

GEM-STONES OF LESSER VALUE.

There are several mineral specimens, besides those mentioned in the previous pages, that have been at one time or another used for ornamental purposes, or for personal adornment, and although these cannot perhaps claim to be strictly precious stones, yet, their consideration cannot well be left out when dealing with gem-stones of a purely ornamental character.

Moonstone.

Taking the feldspar group we find that many of its varieties are used for ornamental purposes, the best known being the moonstone; this is the opalescent variety named adularia, belonging to the orthoclase—feldspar section. The members of this group belong to the monoclinic system (it will be unnecessary to describe this system here, as it is in gems of little importance. It however somewhat resembles the rhombic forms, except that one axis is inclined and not at right angles to the other two axes), and are silicates of alumina and potash; they have a hardness of 6, and a specific gravity of 2·89–2·63, are almost infusible, and are not acted upon by acids. The characteristic physical property of the moonstone is, however, the peculiar chatoyant reflection somewhat resembling that of the cat's-eye, only of a pearly-white colour, and is very marked when the stones are cut *en cabochon*.

The best moonstones come from Ceylon, and are cut in large quantities there. They are not of much value now, although at one time the moonstone was in great request, being "in the fashion." The ancients employed this stone, and used it largely, although it is doubtful whether the feldspar variety is always meant, when the moonstone is referred to in their writings. The name *hecatolite* was given to this stone, because it was thought to enclose the image of Luna, one of the forms of the threefold goddess Hecate. The moonstone of Dioscorides was probably crystallized gypsum or selenite.

Sunstone.

The sunstone is also a member of this group, and is a spangled adularia, containing minute micaceous scales. It is a reddish or golden coloured stone, much darker than the moonstone. It is rarely used in jewellery

Avanturine Feldspar.

The avanturine feldspar contains minute particles of specular or titanic iron, or limonite, disseminated throughout its mass.

Amazon Stone.

Another variety of the orthoclase feldspar occasionally used for ornamental purposes, is the beautiful green mineral called Amazon stone, so named because it was thought to come from the basin of the Amazon, in South America. It used to be obtained from Siberia, but some beautiful specimens have been lately obtained at Pike's Peak, Colorado, in America. The colour is supposed to be due to minute traces of copper, although this has been disputed. Some varieties of amazonite have a spangled appearance, forming a green avanturine in fact.

Labradorite

is another member of the feldspar family, belonging to the triclinic section (it will not be necessary to describe this system), and is a silicate of alumina, lime, and soda. It has a very fine play of colours, and is sometimes used for jewellery; its iridescence is most marked, and it can hardly be mistaken for anything else. As an illustration of the freaks of nature, it may be mentioned that a slab of labradorite, found in Russia, had its constituents arranged in such a manner that a good resemblance was formed of Louis XIV of France, wearing a crown of pomegranate, with a border displaying all the prismatic colours, and a plume of a bluish tint. This natural specimen was owned by a Russian noble, and it is stated that he refused to part with it for 250,000 francs. Labradorite when cut as a gem-stone should not have facets, as its beauty is lost thereby, but it should be cut *en cabochon*. It is in little demand as a gem-stone.

Jade or Green-stone (Nephrite)

is well known in the colonies as "New Zealand green-stone," and is a silicate of magnesia and lime; it is not found crystallized. It is amorphous, massive, compact, tough, and is without cleavage; its hardness is 7, and its specific gravity about 3. It is infusible. It is not much used in Europe for jewellery, although throughout Asia it is a favourite stone. The most colossal and historical of the nephrites (jade) is the stone covering the tomb of Tamerlane. It is composed of two parts, and, according to tradition, became broken during transport. In the border of the higher portion is sculptured in Arabic, an inscription explaining the genealogy of Tamerlane as far as Toumenal Khan. From this description we obtain the exact date of the death of Tamerlane, the 14th of the month Chalbane, of the year 807 of the Hegira. This stone is known to a Mussulman as "Sistap" or "Koche." They attribute to it medicinal powers, and many other mysterious properties. According to the geologist, Mouchetoff, who made special researches into the history of nephrites, and of the localities which produce them, this celebrated stone of Tamerlane comes from the mountains of Khotan; although tradition gives its locality as India.

In New Zealand the natives employed this stone for many purposes of use and adornment, chiefly in the manufacture of their war implements, their axes, and their peculiar club, the *pattoo-pattoo*. This green-stone has been largely used for pendants for the watch-chain, &c., in Australia; perhaps more for its associations than for any real beauty it possesses.

In India, China, and Turkey, jade is carved into dagger and sword handles, cups, and other articles, and these are often inlaid with precious stones. The Indian lapidaries cut the jade with great skill, showing great delicacy of workmanship.

According to Humboldt the Caribees wore jade amulets, cut in the shape of Babylonian cylinders, the origin of which has been the subject of antiquarian research. Dr. Fischer has given much time to the study of this subject, and has endeavoured to prove that the jade objects found in Mexico and Central America were of Asiatic origin, and were brought into America by migration. We know that in the old pile-dwellings in the lakes of Switzerland, polished *celts* or axe-heads have been found made of jade; now no jade is known to occur in the rocks of Europe, but it is plentiful in Turkestan and in some other Eastern localities. The inference is, that these early dwellers in Western Europe, during the stone age, brought their jade with them when they left their Eastern home.

The term jade is a generic one, the scientific name being nephrite, or kidney stone, the stone being considered at one time to be efficacious in diseases of the kidneys.

There is a soft "jade" which is a kind of steatite. The difference in hardness would at once determine this stone. The Rev. J. Milne Curran has notified the occurrence of nephrite in the rocks near Orange in this colony.

Lapis-lazuli

is a stone well-known for its beautiful blue colour, and although largely used in past times for ornamental purposes, yet its chief importance consisted in its permanence as a pigment, which was of the greatest value to the old painters, and to the fact that science has been enabled, from the consideration of its constituents, to manufacture an artificial compound (ultramarine) resembling alike in colour and composition the original mineral. The stone is only used to a small extent for personal adornment, but it has been largely used both in ancient and modern times, for inlay and other architectural work. The Chaldeans and Assyrians employed it with ivory for the decoration of the walls of their palaces; and in the middle ages it was largely used in Europe for the embellishment of ecclesiastical buildings, one of the best examples being the chapel of San Martino, at Naples.

In the Zarskoe Palace, near St. Petersburgh, there is an apartment known as the chamber of Catherine the Second, the walls of which are entirely covered with lapis-lazuli and amber. At the present day it is used in the decoration of furniture and fancy articles, also in the manufacture of studs, brooches, and other articles of jewellery. The colour is a beautiful blue, and the name lazuli is from the Arabic meaning, a blue colour. It is without doubt the sapphire of the ancients. Theophrastus describes it as a blue-stone spotted with gold-dust, and Pliny says it is "like a serene sky adorned with stars, on account of the golden points." The gold mentioned by these ancient writers is yellow iron pyrites, which is often freely distributed throughout the stone, and this, while giving the stone a beautiful appearance, makes it an objectionable one for carving; it was however used for intagli and camei by the Romans. Unfortunately by wear the stones become dull.

The origin of the blue colour is not exactly settled, although many analyses have been made of it. It probably contains sulphur in more than one state of combination (as sulphide and as a sulphate).

The hardness of lapis-lazuli is 5—5'5, and its specific gravity is about 2'4. It is a silicate of alumina, lime and soda, with iron and sodium probably as sulphides. It is usually found in granite rocks, or calcareous limestone, and comes from Persia, China, Siberia, Tartary, Thibet, Europe and Brazil.

Lapis-lazuli occurs in the Baikal Mountains in Siberia, and along the stream Malaya Bystraya, a tributary of the Irkut. In this locality the lapis-lazuli occurs in pockets in the large crystallized dolomitic limestone, near its junction with the syenitic granite. It is of very good quality. From this locality was obtained the lapis-lazuli which served for the veneering of the columns in the St. Isaac Cathedral in St. Petersburg, and also for decorating portions of the Imperial palaces.

The value of the finest stones, of a deep blue colour, and without admixture of foreign constituents, is, according to Emanuel, 10s. to 50s. per ounce, according to the size of the piece. In olden times when it was in much request for the manufacture of ultramarine, fragments of it were worth 10 crowns a pound, and when very good this quantity would supply 10 ounces of ultramarine, which is perhaps the most permanent pigment ever discovered.

Lapis-lazuli has not yet been found in this Colony.

Iolite or Dichroite

which is occasionally cut and polished as a gemstone, is known by the term *Saphir d'eau.* We must admit that one of the most important, pleasing, and striking qualities of ornamental stones is their colour, of course always excepting colourless diamonds and stones of that character, and from a scientific point of view, these coloured stones afford some of the most interesting phenomena with which we are acquainted.

The property possessed by some minerals of displaying different colours when viewed in different directions, and known as *pleochroism*, is very marked in iolite and it has on this account, received its other name *dichroite.* Crystals of this mineral, when viewed in the direction of the vertical axis, appearing deep blue while at right angles to this axis they exhibit a pale blue and yellowish hue. When seen in the dichroiscope, the two squares are pale buff and indigo blue.

Iolite belongs to the rhombic system, has a hardness of 7—7·5 and a specific gravity of 2·6—2·7. It is a silicate of alumina, magnesia, and iron, and is with difficulty fusible on the edges, this property distinguishing it from stones it otherwise somewhat resembles. It is of course softer than the sapphire, although it has been mistaken for that gem. The best specimens come from Ceylon, the home of so many of the better gem-stones. Unfortunately many of the specimens are full of flaws, and those which are found in Bavaria are sometimes almost opaque. Fair specimens are also found in America. Iolite refers to "violet," and dichroite signifies "two colours." There is another blue mineral named *kyanite*, that might be mistaken for iolite, and which is occasionally used for jewellery. It has even been sold for the sapphire, although this should be easily decided, as its hardness is always less than 7. It is a silicate of alumina, and has a specific gravity 3·6 —3·7. It is, however, but little used as a gem-stone.

Crocidolite.

This stone belongs to the amphibole or hornblende group of minerals, and is allied to asbestos. By alteration of the contained protoxide of iron it assumes a golden fibrous appearance, but the alteration has not stopped here, as South African specimens often have a chalcedonic base, a hardness of nearly 7, a specific gravity of 3, and are essentially pseudomorphs. It is one of the innumerable minerals named "cat's-eye," and when cut *en cabochon* with a high ridge, it presents a brilliant appearance; this chatoyant appearance is, as has been seen, common to all this class of minerals possessing a fibrous structure. The true "cat's-eye" is a beautiful gem, many times more valuable than crocidolite, and it is misleading to attach this name to inferior stones. The golden appearance is very marked in some specimens of crocidolite, and the fibrous structure is very characteristic. I saw, a short time back, a gentleman wearing a watch chain made of plates of crocidolite, mounted in gold, and connected together by links. The appearance, although striking, was too gaudy to be effective, and it is hardly probable that this material will come into general use for articles of this character. It would be most suitable for the decoration of small articles for use rather than ornament. No doubt the desire to wear this stone is more for its associations than for real ornament. The same inclination is also seen in the practice of wearing small "nuggets" of gold, mounted on a ring or a pin, so common among the gold diggers of this Colony. The "green-stone" pendants, so frequently worn attached to the watch chain, may also be mentioned as illustrating the prevalence of this sentiment. Good specimens of crocidolite are found on the Orange River in South Africa, also in Norway, Greenland, and India.

The name is from *krokus*, meaning wool, and the correct name should be as it is sometimes written, *krokydolite.*

There are a few other silicates which have occasionally been used for gem-stones, but without any marked success. Among these we may mention *axinite,* a mineral belonging to the triclinic system, and having a hardness of about 7, but it is very brittle, and on this account little used as a gem-stone. It looks well, however, when cut *en cabochon.* It is generally brownish in colour, and strongly pleiochroic. It is of importance from a scientific point of view, as being the only mineral used as a gem-stone, with the exception of tourmaline, containing the element boron. The name signifies an axe, and was given to it in allusion to the form of the crystals, these being usually thin and sharp-edged. It fuses readily before the blow-pipe.

Euclase.

This stone was first brought to Europe from South America in 1785, but it has been obtained since from the Ural Mountains. The name was given by Haüy, and means "easy to break," because of its brittle nature, a defect that has prevented its use in any quantity as a gem-stone, although its hardness is 7·5, is fairly transparent, and takes a good polish. In its chemical composition it is somewhat allied to the emerald (containing glucina), although crystallizing in a different system—the monoclinic. It has also a higher specific gravity. It is generally of a straw-colour, passing into green and blue. It has a fine lustre. At its home in the neighbourhood of Villa Rica, Brazil, it is associated with topaz in a chloritic schist.

The remaining silicates that have been cut for gems are of little importance, both from a commercial and historical point of view, with, perhaps, the exception of *hiddenite,* a variety of spodumene, found in Alexander County, North Carolina, U.S.A. It was named after the discoverer, Mr. W. E. Hidden, of New York, who leased the ground from the owner, and carried on a systematic exploration in 1880, which resulted in finding the mineral *in situ,* it having been previously found in loose crystals, sparsely scattered over the surface of the soil. It is a beautiful green stone, and is known as "lithia-emerald." It has a hardness of 7, a specific gravity of 3, and crystallizes in the monoclinic system. When cut and polished it resembles the emerald in brilliancy, transparency, and lustre, although of a less beautiful colour than that gem. When first discovered and introduced, it had a large sale, perhaps because of the novelty of being purely an American gem. For some time the demand exceeded the supply; a 2½-carat stone was sold for £100, and a number of stones were sold from £8 to over £20 a carat. The finest crystal found of "lithia-emerald" measures 2¾ in. x ¼ in. x ½ in. and would cut a gem-stone weighing about 5¼ carats. Now that the novelty has worn off, it is generally admitted that these gems can never supersede the emerald in public estimation; but the success which they met with was thoroughly deserved by those who by their persistent efforts unearthed this treasure.

Spodumene is a silicate of alumina and lithia, containing about 6 per cent. of the latter, and before the blow-pipe swells up and fuses to a clear glass, colouring the flame a bright crimson.

Malachite

is a hydrous carbonate of copper, having a green colour, and belongs to a different class of minerals that have been used for ornamental purposes, both in ancient and modern times. It is mostly found massive or incrusting, and with a smooth mammilated or botryoidal surface. The different green colours are usually distributed in a banded concentric manner; these bands showing successive deposits of the mineral, and have in most cases resulted from the percolation of water through copper-bearing rocks, and the subsequent deposition of the dissolved carbonate of copper.

Although it has been very largely used for decorative work and small ornamental articles, it is too soft to be of much value for jewellery, having a hardness of 3·5—4, a specific gravity, 3·7—4, and crystallizing in the monoclinic system when thus found. It dissolves with effervescence in acids (presence of carbonic acid), and when heated on charcoal is reduced to metallic copper.

Theophrastus states that a species of stone comes from the copper-mines, and is called false emerald. This most probably refers to our malachite. The *molochites* of Pliny, obtained from Arabia, having a deep green colour, and nearly opaque, is also probably our malachite. The name malachite is from *moloche* or *malache*, meaning marsh-mallow, and refers to its green colour.

The finest specimens come from Nijni-Tagilsk in Siberia, from mines belonging to the late Prince Demidoff. One block from this locality was obtained measuring 16 feet long, 7½ feet wide, and 8½ feet thick, of very good quality. The exhibit from this locality at the London Exhibition of 1851, consisting of doors and vases, created quite a sensation, and directed public attention to this material for decorative work. In Russia, furniture and household fittings are often covered with veneer made of malachite, and in the collection at St. Petersburg there is a mass of 3½ feet square, of a fine emerald green colour, weighing 90 lb., and stated to be worth £82,000. At Versailles there is a room, the furniture and ornaments of which are of malachite. There are many other ornamental works of historic interest made of this material, but it is not likely that its use will become general.

Besides the Russian localities, some fine specimens have been obtained at the Burra Burra mines of South Australia, and it is common in many other countries. Some very delicate specimens of this mineral have been obtained at the Cobar mines of this Colony, but not fit for ornamental purposes.

Iron Pyrites

Was largely used for jewellery during the eighteenth century, and although taking a fine polish, is of very little value. It was used by the ancient Mexicans with turquoise and obsidian for decorative purposes.

Forms of cutting Precious Stones.

IT would not perhaps be advisable to conclude without some description of the various methods used in the fashioning of rough stones into the symmetrical and beautiful finished article; and also without a brief description of the mode of buying and selling, and the manufacture of artificial and imitation gems.

In their rough state the qualities of lustre, refraction, and dispersion of light, so much prized in precious stones, are but ill-displayed. To bring out these properties to their highest perfection it has been found necessary to form these irregular stones into symmetrical ones, by grinding and polishing smooth faces or facets upon them, or as it is termed, "cut them." An illustration of the principal forms into which precious stones are cut is seen in the accompanying plate.

To bring out the most beautiful form, it is often necessary to reduce the size to a great extent, half the stone being occasionally removed to secure a perfect gem, and it may be considered that in the cutting of large diamonds about half the stone will be removed. The "Star of the South," a Brazilian diamond, weighed in the rough 254½ carats, and when cut 125 carats. The "Regent" or "Pitt" diamond, weighed 410 carats in the rough, and when cut it was reduced to 136⅞ carats, so that in these two instances we see the enormous amount of material sacrificed for the sake of mere beauty. Oriental nations were satisfied to allow the stone to be one of size rather than beauty, and were not so fastidious as to sacrifice quantity to quality. The unsymmetrical contour of the "Koh-i-noor" when it first arrived in England is sufficient illustration of this fact; the two principal planes indeed being cleavage planes, and besides it had two or three flaws remaining, which might have been a serious defect, and cause the breaking of the stone; these were successfully removed in the recutting. There were also two notches cut in the stone for the purpose of holding it in its original setting. By the presence of these large cleavage planes it is very probable that the Koh-i-noor was only a portion of a larger stone, perhaps the original "Mountain of Light."

Tavernier, who was himself a celebrated authority on gems, wrote a book of his travels, published in Paris in 1676, in which he gives an account of a celebrated diamond, the "Great Mogul," supposed to have been at that time the largest diamond ever found, its original weight uncut being 787½ carats. When he saw it, it had been cut, and the weight reduced to 279½ carats. Now all trace of this celebrated diamond has been lost, and it has been the subject of very great discussion whether the Koh-i-noor is not a portion of this original gigantic gem. Dr. Beke, in a paper read before the British Association, at Ipswich, in 1851, says, that at the capture of Coochan there was found among the jewels of the harem of Reeza Kooli Khan, the chief of that place, a large diamond slab, supposed to have been cut or broken from one side of the Koh-i-noor, the great Indian diamond in the possession of Her Majesty. It weighed about 130 carats, and on the flat side appeared to correspond with the Koh-i-noor. According to particulars gathered respecting this "slab" of diamond, it appears that it was taken from a poor man, a native of Khorassan, in whose family it had served for striking light

FORMS OF CUTTING PRECIOUS STONES

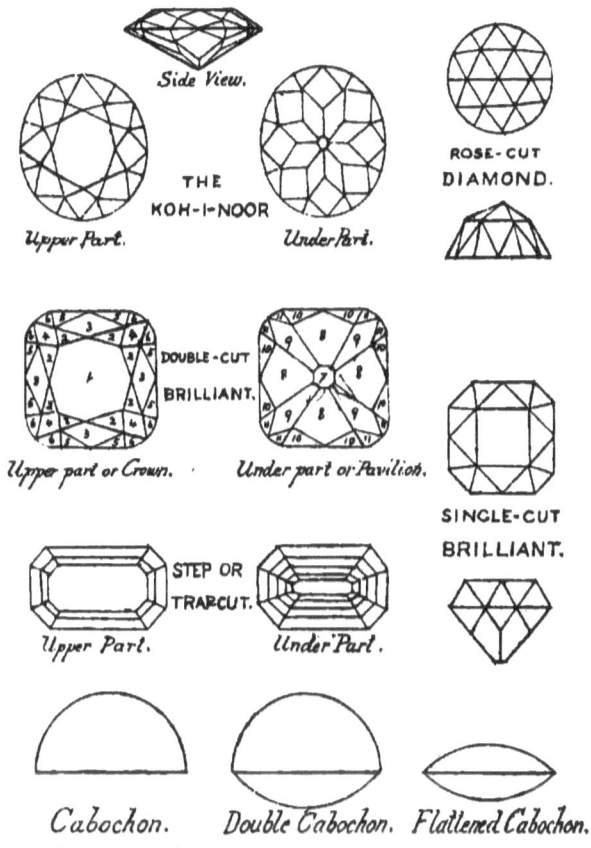

Side View.

THE
KOH-I-NOOR

Upper Part.

Under Part.

ROSE-CUT
DIAMOND.

DOUBLE-CUT
BRILLIANT.

Upper part or Crown.

Under part or Pavilion.

SINGLE-CUT
BRILLIANT.

STEP OR
TRAPCUT.

Upper Part.

Under Part.

Cabochon.

Double Cabochon.

Flattened Cabochon.

(5 e 201-95-6)

against a steel in the place of flint, and one side of it was a good deal worn by constant use. The price asked by the Armenian jewellers to cut this stone was equivalent to £10,000 of our money, giving an idea of the enormous labour necessary to fashion the diamond by the appliances in use by these lapidaries. This stone is now presumed to be among the Crown jewels of Persia. It is the gem known as the "Abbas Mīrza." Another diamond which singularly corresponds with the Koh-i-noor is the great Russian diamond, and it is not improbable, says Prof. Tennant, that they all three formed one crystal—perhaps a rhombic dodecahedron—and together would make up the original weight as given by Tavernier, allowing for detached pieces splintered off in the process of cleaving.

The portion now so beautifully cut, and which forms one of the Crown jewels of England, was worn by its former owner, Runject Sing, as an armlet. The Hon. W. G. Osborne, in describing a visit to this potentate, says:— "Crossed-legged in a golden chair sat Runjeet Sing, dressed in simple white, wearing no ornament but a single string of enormous pearls round his waist, and the celebrated Koh-i-noor on his arm." On the annexation of the Punjab it was given up to the East India Company for the Queen of England, and was taken to London in 1850. It had then little beauty, judged by European ideas, and it was necessary to cut it into the form of a "brilliant." It weighed 186$\frac{1}{16}$ carats, and it now weighs 102$\frac{1}{16}$ carats, over 83 carats being removed in the process of recutting. The exact representation is given in the plate, and is taken from a glass model in the Technological Museum collection. A model of the Koh-i-noor before recutting is also displayed in the same case.

The recutting of this gem was commenced on July 16th, 1852, his Grace the late Duke of Wellington first placing it on the mill, a horizontal iron plate made to revolve up to 3,000 revolutions per minute, diamond powder being used as the abrading substance. The diamond was fixed in pewter to enable it to be pressed upon the plate. It was found to be very hard in places—so hard, in fact, that the medium rate of 2,400 revolutions per minute continued for six hours made little impression upon it, and the speed had to be increased to more than 3,000 revolutions. The hardness was of that character that the diamond became at one time so hot from the continued friction and greater weight applied that it melted the pewter setting, and it is stated that at another time the particles of iron mixed with the diamond powder and oil became ignited. The stone was finished on September 7th, having taken thirty-eight days to cut, working twelve hours a day without intermission. The cost of recutting was about £8,000. The cost of cutting the "Regent" or "Pitt" diamond was about £5,000, and the time taken was two years, the difference in time being that the "Regent" was cut by manual labour and the "Koh-i-noor" by steam power. The "Star of the South" took three months to cut.

The art of gem polishing has been practised in Europe for a very long time. As early as 1290 a guild was formed in Paris, and in 1373 the profession was carried on at Nuremburg. The seat of the gem-cutting industry was shifted from one city to another, according to circumstances, during the succeeding centuries. At one time, through religious intolerance, the Jewish merchants left Lisbon, and settled in Holland, and thus established an industry in the same manner as the Huguenots introduced the weaving industry into England. The centre of the diamond trade was thus in the sixteenth century fixed at Amsterdam, and it remains to-day the principal seat of the diamond-cutting industry, 10,000 of its inhabitants being connected with the business in one way or another.

There are three operations in the cutting and polishing of the diamond, which in large establishments are carried out by special workmen, because in this industry, as in all others, an individual by constant application to any particular branch becomes most expert, and by this division of labour the greatest advantage arises in the saving of material, time, and money. These three operations are *splitting, cutting,* and *polishing.*

The splitter fashions the rough stone into its proper form, allowing for the greatest weight and brilliant effect possible from the individual stone, and removing flaws and imperfections with the least possible waste. The mode of splitting is to cut a notch with another diamond corrresponding to a cleavage plane of the diamond to be split, inserting a blunt instrument into the notch, and removing the desired piece by striking a blow with a wooden baton. The pieces removed are often worked up into cut gems.

The stone then passes into the hands of the cutter, who cements two stones into wooden handles and grinds the two together, thus grinding a facet of the two stones at once, or illustrating the oft-quoted remark of " Diamond cut diamond."

After the cutter has brought the diamond to the required shape and fashioned it with its required number of facets, it is passed on to be polished. The diamonds are for this process cemented into metal, and then polished with diamond dust and oil upon steel disks revolving at an enormous speed (two thousand revolutions per minute). These disks revolve horizontally, and quite true.

The diamond powder used in the cutting is prepared from " Bort," or faulty diamonds, and pieces splintered off, the greatest care being taken to preserve the smallest particle. These are put into a mortar of hardened steel, and hammered until fine enough for use, the perfect cleavage of the diamond materially assisting the process.

The different forms into which precious stones are cut may be arranged into two groups, those having plane surfaces and those having curved surfaces.

1. Plane surfaces
{
Brilliant-cut.
Step or trap-cut.
Table-cut.
Rose-cut.
}

2. Curved surfaces
{
Single cabochon.
Double   „
Hollowed „
Flattened „
}

The brilliant-cut and the rose-cut are usually adopted for the diamond, and occasionally the table-cut. The step or trap-cut is used for the emerald and stones of that description, usually found in prisms. The different forms of the cabochon are used for brittle stones, and gems of the moonstone character ; while the flattened cabochon is much used for the opal, and called "tallow-topped." When the garnet is cut *en cabochon* it is often hollowed at the back to make the stone thinner, on account of the dark colour of the "carbuncle."

By referring to the figure of the double-cut brilliant in the plate, it will be seen that there are 58 facets, 33 of which are in the " crown" or upper part of the brilliant, and 25 in the " pavilion " or lower part. This form of cutting was invented by Peruzzi, of Venice, during the reign of Louis XIII of France.

The brilliant often takes a more circular form than that shown, and, as in the Koh-i-noor, eight "star" facets are cut round the "culet," making the stone to have 66 facets. Referring to the numbers in the plate, the names of the facets in technical terms are as follows, the numbers corresponding with those in the figures :—

Crown or Upper part
- 1. The table.
- 2. Eight-star facets.
- 3. Four templets or bezils.
- 4. Four quoins or lozenges.
- 5. Eight cross or skew facets.
- 6. Eight skill facets.

Pavilion or Under part
- 7. The culet or collet.
- 8. Four pavilion facets.
- 9. Four quoins.
- 10. Eight cross facets.
- 11. Eight skill facets.

The "girdle" is that portion of the stone of greatest diameter, and is used to fix the brilliant in its setting. Certain rules have also been laid down, so that the greatest effect may be obtained, but it is not always possible to adhere too strongly to these rules. Two notable instances may be mentioned where these laws have been deviated from : the Koh-i-noor, which is thinner, and the Regent or Pitt, which is thicker than ordinary.

The single-cut brilliant is the old form of cutting.

The rose-cut has been in use since the year 1520, and although giving good effect, yet it is deficient to the former. If the stone bears 24 facets, as in the plate, it is a "Holland rose;" if 18 facets, a "semi-Holland;" if less it is an "Antwerp rose." It will be understood that to cut a brilliant the stone must have a certain thickness, while a "rose" can be manufactured from pieces that are too thin to make brilliants. It has been stated that rose diamonds have been cut so minute that several hundreds only weigh one carat. The rose-cut diamond is much less expensive than the brilliant.

It appears that diamonds several centuries ago were cut with a square or oblong plane on both sides ; they were termed "table" or "Indian-cut," probably taking advantage of the cleavage of the diamond. There are other forms of cutting, which take advantage of the contour of the stone, as in the "Sancy" and the "Orloff."

Mode of Buying and Selling.

THE trade in diamonds represents, perhaps, 90 per cent. of the capital invested in precious stones, and there is not much likelihood of diamonds depreciating in value at present, or the large amount obtained at the mines of South Africa during late years would have had the effect of much cheapening them, as the quantity taken from these mines since their discovery is reckoned by tons, and as the output is likely to be regulated, prices will probably be maintained.

Many fluctuations in the value of diamonds have taken place during the present century, brought about by extraordinary circumstances; as when Dom Pedro paid the interest of the Brazilian State debt to England in diamonds; and again in consequence of the French Revolution in 1848, and other like instances. In 1750 the value of a diamond, based on the brilliant and weighing 1 carat, was £8, a gem of 2 carats £32, one of 4 carats £128, and so on. This rule is from the tables of David Jeffries, although it has been traced to 100 years before, and is based on the square of the weight of the diamond in carats multiplied by 8, the value in pounds of 1 carat; for example, a stone of 2 carats, 2 × 2 × 8 = £32. There appears to have been no other tables yet compiled, and although this mode of calculation gives a rough value, yet it is not followed now, as the value of small brilliants of 1 to 4 carats has increased out of all proportion to the gems of greater weight, a perfect gem of 1 carat being valued at nearly three times as much. It is almost impossible to value a diamond by its weight alone, as so much depends upon the colour, brilliancy, and cutting of the gem. Diamonds of absolute purity, clear as water, and free from all blemish, are called of the "first water," only about 8 per cent. of those found being of this quality, while 25 per cent. are of the second quality. Some authorities give the percentage of the best stones as higher than here given.

The Carat and Sale of Gems.

Precious stones are purchased by a weight called a *carat*, a word probably derived from a seed, of which there are several that have nearly constant weights, and are native in India. The scarlet and black leguminous seed *Abrus precatorius* weighs about 2 grains, the seed of *Adenanthera pavonina* about 4 grains, while that of the locust tree, *Ceratonia siliqua*, weighs about 3⅛ grains. At one time the carat was not the same weight in all countries, the international carat is equal to ·205 gram., or about 3·164 troy grains. Thus an English ounce troy equals nearly 152 carats. Originally the carat was considered equal to 4 grains, but when spoken of now as equalling that amount it means diamond grains, and has no reference to either troy or avoirdupois weights.

Imitation Gems.

THE art of making imitation precious stones has reached a high state of perfection, and there is in the Technological Museum a remarkably good set of these " paste " gems. The manufacture has been carried on for a very great number of years, and no doubt often with great profit, as many of the supposed gems which used to embellish European churches are without doubt " paste." The imitation gems are usually made of a material called *strass*, composed principally of the very best glass, with a large percentage of lead to give lustre, and different metallic oxides to impart colour, as cobalt for the sapphire, chromium for the emerald, &c. Their detection is not difficult, as they are comparatively soft, all yielding to a file ; have a high specific gravity, and are not dichroic like many real gems.

Artificial Gems.

A DISTINCTION must be made between *imitation* and *artificial* gems; the latter are made by taking the same component parts as are contained in the real gem, and then by great heat or other methods, forming a stone having the same composition, hardness, and crystalline form as the real gem. As yet marketable stones of the most valuable gems have not been made, although minute diamonds, rubies, and sapphires have been artificially manufactured, and good sized spinels have also been made, which could not be distinguished from natural stones. The tendency of the higher chemistry to-day is towards synthesis rather than analysis, and the progress of the science will no doubt overcome the problem of the manufacture of the better class gems, of saleable size and quality. It is problematical whether the diamond will be made of sufficiently large size to be of value commercially, although from a scientific point of view the making artificially of the minute octahedron of crystallized carbon, is an accomplishment one may well be proud of, especially as it breaks down another barrier between the scientist and the secrets of the laboratory of Nature.

81

INDEX.

	PAGE.
Abbas Mirza diamond	75
Adamantine spar	29
Agate	60
,, artificial staining of	61
,, banded	60
,, brecciated	60
,, clouded	60
,, composition of	60
,, fantastic forms of	61
,, fortification	60
,, historical	61
,, jasper	60
,, mode of cutting	61
,, moss	60
,, New South Wales localities	62
,, onyx	60
,, opal	50
,, ribbon	60
,, uses of	60
,, where cut and polished	61
,, where found	61
,, wood	61
,, zone	60
Alexandrite	44
,, dichroism of	44
,, where found	44
Almandine or precious garnet	35
,, ruby—violet spinel	31
Amazon stone	68
,, colour of	68
,, where found	68
Amethyst	59
,, alteration of colour by heating	60
,, geological formation	60
,, historical	59
,, meaning of term	59
,, mode of cutting	59
,, New South Wales localities	60
,, scarabei	59
,, where found	60
,, value of	59
Andradite	36
Aplome	36
Aquamarine	28
,, engraved	28
,, historical	28
,, Oriental	19, 25
,, value of	28
,, where found	28
Artificial gems	79
,, ruby	23, 79
Ashes-drawer	54

	PAGE.
Asteria	25
,, how cut	26
,, value of	26
Australian rubies, garnets	22, 37
Austrian yellow diamond	17
Avanturine	67
,, artificial	67
,, feldspar	68
,, where found	67
Axinite	72
,, meaning of term	72
Balas ruby—rose-red spinel	31
Barklyite	22
Beryl	27
,, cleavage of	27
,, colours of	27
,, commercial value of	28
,, composition of	27
,, crystalline system of	27
,, lustre of	27
,, size of crystals	27, 28
,, specific gravity of	27
,, varieties of	27, 28, 29
,, where found	28
Bingera diamonds	13
,, geological formation	13
,, where found	13
Black garnet	36
Bloodstone	64
Blue beryl	27, 28
Blue beryl in Crown of England	28
Blue sapphire	23
Blue tourmaline	53
Bohemian garnet	35
Bone turquois	53
Borneo diamonds	12
Bort or Boort	11
Brazilian diamonds	12
,, emerald	53
,, ruby	53
,, sapphire	53
,, topaz	38
Bristol diamonds	56
Bultfontein Mine, South Africa	12
Burnt topaz	38
Cairngorm—brown quartz crystal	58
Californian diamonds	56
Cameos	48

F

[Illustrations.]

Sydney : Charles Potter, Government Printer.—1896.

www.ingramcontent.com/pod-product-compliance
Lightning Source LLC
Chambersburg PA
CBHW032151010726
47493CB00008BA/2651